"Is there somebody there?"

Nobody answered.

Owen lay the flowers against Sara's headstone, feeling the engraving under his fingertips.

Corporal Marissa "Sara" Jenkins-Kilpatrick

Canadian Armed Forces

"Owen?"

He heard his late wife's voice calling his name.

Was he hearing things?

He looked up and there stood Sara, in a long dress and boots, with wisps of black hair streaming out from under a disheveled bonnet.

A sob caught in his throat as his mind struggled to understand what his eyes were seeing.

His estranged wife was dead, buried in a coffin in the soil beneath him. And yet, as Owen pushed himself to his feet, he found himself calling her name. "Sara? Is that you?"

"Yes!" she called. He heard fear, joy and relief mingling in her voice. "I'm in trouble and I need your help."

Maggie K. Black is an award-winning journalist and romantic suspense author with an insatiable love of traveling the world. She has lived in the American South, Europe and the Middle East. She now makes her home in Canada with her history-teacher husband, their two beautiful girls and a small but mighty dog. Maggie enjoys connecting with her readers at maggiekblack.com.

Books by Maggie K. Black

Love Inspired Suspense

Undercover Protection
Surviving the Wilderness
Her Forgotten Life

Rocky Mountain K-9 Unit

Explosive Revenge

Protected Identities

Christmas Witness Protection
Runaway Witness
Christmas Witness Conspiracy

True North Heroes

Undercover Holiday Fiancée
The Littlest Target
Rescuing His Secret Child
Cold Case Secrets

Visit the Author Profile page at LoveInspired.com for more titles.

HER FORGOTTEN LIFE

MAGGIE K. BLACK

LOVE INSPIRED SUSPENSE
INSPIRATIONAL ROMANCE

LOVE INSPIRED® SUSPENSE
INSPIRATIONAL ROMANCE

ISBN-13: 978-1-335-58745-9

Recycling programs
for this product may
not exist in your area.

Her Forgotten Life

Love Inspired
22 Adelaide St. West, 41st Floor
Toronto, Ontario M5H 4E3, Canada
www.LoveInspired.com

Printed in U.S.A.

Yet will I not forget thee.
Behold, I have graven thee upon the palms of my hands.
—*Isaiah* 49:15-16

A beloved member of my found family
died while I was writing this book.

She hated romance novels and
never read a single one of mine.

But she loved me, I loved her and I will miss her.

So this book is for all those we love yet disagree with.

May those things that unite us
always be greater than those which divide.

ONE

Sara awoke to the sound of floorboards creaking somewhere below her in the Zook family's Ontario Amish *haus*. She sat up straight in her old wooden bed and listened. At least two sets of footsteps were creeping across the floor. Terror pounded through her heart. She'd been there on her own for the past few days, after the Zooks had left to visit family in Pennsylvania Dutch country. But she wasn't alone anymore. Somebody else was there. Were thieves prowling the remote Amish farmhouse to see what they could steal?

Or had whoever tried to murder her six months ago finally found her?

She steeled a breath, prayed and waited. Silence fell from the floor below her. But still a sense of unease lingered in her core. Had she imagined it, or was there really someone in the house with her? She didn't know which idea scared her more. With shaking fingers, she lit the small oil lamp that sat on her bedside table. There were no clocks to tell her the time, but the pale January light told her it was just before dawn. Her limbs trembled while her mind still swam with confusing fragments of the recurring nightmare she'd just been jolted out of.

In her dreams, she'd been running for her life. Her head had been ablaze with pain, and she'd been so scared she could barely breathe. An indistinct, loud and terrifying roar sounded behind her. She started falling down a steep embankment. Then suddenly she was lying in a hospital bed and a baby was crying. And then she was with an *Englischer* man with kind green eyes and hair the color of a farmland sunset.

She blinked the images away, rose from her bed and crept toward the door. Disjointed scraps of her former life had haunted the corners of her amnesiac mind ever since the night an elderly farmer named Petrus Zook had pulled her battered body from a nearby river six months ago and brought her home to be slowly nursed back to health by his wife, Hadassah, with the help of his brother, Dr. Amos Zook.

For the first few weeks, Sara had been plagued by headaches that were so strong she could barely move or open her eyes, let alone walk. Petrus had called the Ontario Provincial Police from the communal phone in the middle of the village, but no one had been reported missing who matched her description. Her black hair had been short back then, and when Dr. Amos had stitched up the nasty gash on the back of her head, he'd told Sara that not only did she have a severe concussion, but he also suspected she'd been nicked by a bullet. The idea she'd been shot was even more terrifying than the fear of not knowing who she was. As she'd grown stronger and gotten back on her feet, Sara had spent her days helping them out around the farm as much as she was able and praying to *Gott* they'd be spared from whatever danger had stolen her memories and almost taken her life.

But now Petrus and Hadassah were gone, having left on a long trek to visit an ailing relative on the other side of the border in Pennsylvania Dutch Country for a few weeks. They'd wanted to take her with them, but of course she couldn't cross the US border without identification, and she'd assured them she'd be fine. Dr. Amos had invited Sara to move in with his wife and children until their return, but she'd wanted to repay Petrus and Hadassah's kindness by staying at their home to care for their horses and farm.

A rhythmic banging began to sound below her, as if someone was trying to break in. Or maybe it was just the wind tossing the front door open and then slamming it back against the hinges. The injury that had stolen her memories still sometimes played tricks on her mind. Either way, she couldn't just stay in her room and cower.

Sara's hands shook as she put on and pinned a simple calf-length dress with thick leggings and wool socks underneath, tied her now shoulder-length black hair back and slid a fresh white *kapp* over it. The *Englischer* jeans and shirt she'd been wearing when they'd found her had been so caked in mud it was hard to tell what their original shape and color had been, but knowing Hadassah, she'd probably kept them somewhere for her in case she ever wanted them again. The only other thing she'd had on her, besides the clothes on her back, had been a golden ring on a chain around her neck, on which three words were engraved: *Sara Owen Kilpatrick*.

Now that gold chain hung, as always, around her

neck with the ring nestled against her heart. While those who followed the *Ordnung*, which governed what the Amish called *plain* life, didn't wear jewelry, she always felt safest knowing she had it there, tucked under her clothes, as her only link to who she was.

When the Zooks had asked if her name was Sara, somehow she'd known the answer was yes.

Apparently Kilpatrick was the name of a small Canadian town about a day away by horse and buggy. But when Dr. Amos had brought over pictures of the town, which someone at the hospital where he consulted had kindly printed off their computer for him, she hadn't recognized anything in them. They also hadn't found any records of a Sara or Owen Kilpatrick living in Ontario. As they hadn't known who attacked Sara and what she needed protection from, they hadn't wanted to contact random people with that last name just in case they accidentally tipped off her abuser to her location—or even to the fact she was still alive.

And yet, something inside her told her that Owen was the name of the man whose face she'd seen in her dreams.

But if so, why hadn't he reported her missing or tried to find her?

Darkness loomed around her as she opened the door and looked out. She took the lamp from her bedside table and dimmed it until the light was barely more than the faintest glow and started down the hallway. Her stockinged feet moved silently across the wooden floor. The wide staircase was at the end of the hall, and she started down it cautiously, one step at a time.

The large main living room came into view, with Hadassah's beautiful handmade quilts draped lovingly over Petrus's handcrafted furniture. Sara had worked on a couple of those quilts too while she was recovering from whatever ordeal had landed her here. Last month, she'd even accompanied Hadassah to the local holiday market to help her sell them.

The sound of things crashing came from somewhere out of view, along with the sound of glass shattering. It sounded like someone was ransacking the kitchen, throwing the contents of the cupboard onto the floor.

Were they looking for something? Were they looking for her?

Her long lace-up boots and coat lay straight ahead beside the front door. There were warm gloves and a scarf tucked inside her jacket pocket. She could hide somewhere and pray whoever had broken in would take what they were after and leave. Or, if she was fast enough, she could grab her coat and boots, sprint to the barn, get on one of the Zook family horses and escape.

But even as the thought crossed her mind, somehow she knew her only choice was to run.

Furtively, she scanned the room. It was empty. She could only hear one intruder, and he was still in the kitchen. She took a long, deep breath and ran for the door. Her feet slid into the boots. Pausing to lace them up would have to wait. She grabbed the coat off a hook, juggled the lamp from one hand to another and shoved her arms through the sleeves, then flung open the door.

A heavyset man in a dark ski mask blocked her path. His eyes narrowed.

"Yo, Beau!" he shouted. "There's a woman in the house!"

A male voice she assumed was Beau's swore from

the kitchen. "Grab her!" Beau snapped. "We can't let anybody know we were here!"

The masked man lunged for her. His large hands grabbed for her arm. She wrenched herself from his grasp, turned and ran back into the house. A second masked man charged at her through the kitchen door. She sprinted up the stairs, hearing both men on her tail. Her feet reached the landing, and she started down the hall, but before she'd taken two steps, she felt rough hands grab her coat and yank her back. She swung back hard and caught him on the side of the head with her oil lamp. He swore and let go. She darted into her bedroom, slammed the door and then shoved the wooden dresser over so that it toppled to the floor in front of it.

But it wouldn't hold them long.

Sara ran to the shutters and pushed them open. Freezing air rushed in through the window. Deep snow, almost four feet high, spread out beneath her in unblemished waves of silvery white, leading to the thick forest of trees. Sara extinguished the lamp, took three steps back then sprinted straight toward the window. Her right hand brushed the frame as she leaped through without hesitation. Her body tumbled through the air toward the soft cushion of snow. Instinctively, she braced herself for impact then hit the ground and sank deep.

In an instant, she was back on her feet. She turned toward the barn, but the door was open and the horses were gone. She ran past it, through the snow and toward the shelter of the trees. Thick flakes swirled down around her, landing on her cheeks, where the cold mingled with her own hot tears. Thankfully the falling snow would help obscure her escape and bury her trail.

Questions filled her mind. How had she known how to jump and fall like that? Who was she? What had those men been looking for?

Where would she go now?

The scent of smoke reached her senses as she stepped into the trees. Sara looked back. Red and orange flames licked high through the billowing smoke where her refuge had once stood. The farmhouse was on fire.

She reached for the ring she wore around her neck. Her fingertips ran over the engraving.

Sara Owen Kilpatrick.

She was out of options with nowhere left to run.

She'd make her way to Kilpatrick and search for answers.

Somehow, she'd find Owen.

A smattering of fireworks erupted in the dark night sky above Mayor Patrick "Owen" Kilpatrick's head, illuminating the winter's gloom as he drove the snowmobile he'd custom-built down Main Street in the small Northern Ontario town that bore his family's name. He was a fifth generation Kilpatrick, most of whom were named some variation of "Patrick" and so went by their middle names. It had been several days since New Year's Eve had come and gone. But judging by both the cheers and music that rose from Roger Wilson's legal office, the man who would soon take over from Owen as the new mayor was throwing one big hoot and holler of a shindig.

Owen had been invited to the party, of course. And judging by the glimpses he caught through the window, almost every single pillar of the community and small business owner in town was there—from the florist to the dentist to the bakery owner. He fixed his eyes instead on the church perched on a small hill at the end of the town and, beyond it, the family cemetery, where he was going. He was headed to the graveyard to lay flowers on the grave of the only woman he'd ever loved.

He moved slowly past the charming storefronts, with their stained glass windows and snow-covered awnings. Small towns like Kilpatrick were a dying breed in rural Canada, and through the shield of his helmet's visor, the scene was picturesque and beautiful, especially with the falling snow and backdrop of the blue-black sky. But Owen's heart was so heavy inside his chest he could barely breathe.

Was he the only one who realized the town he loved was on the edge of disaster?

Flyers in every window advertised the upcoming winter fair, and he knew that was all anybody would be talking about at the party. And not just because it would end with Roger's swearing in as mayor. Owen had grown up in this town and gone to that fair—the town's pride and joy—every year since he was born.

His grandfather had been mayor, like his father before him. Owen's uncle had been mayor by the time Owen moved away to Ottawa to bounce between college programs trying to find himself. Owen's cousin had taken over two years ago, before dying in a tragic hit-and-run less than a year ago.

As the last remaining Kilpatrick, Owen had suddenly inherited both a good chunk of the land that the town was on and a deep feeling of responsibility to care for all of it. That was when Owen had returned home, reopened the town hardware store and moved into the small one-bedroom apartment above it. He'd also stepped in as temporary mayor and discovered the town was not only broke but clinging to the success of the annual fair to keep itself from bankruptcy.

But what could he do?

Owen had his own world of problems.

His marriage to Sara had fallen apart, and he'd already been staying on a friend's couch. Moving out permanently seemed to be best for both of them. All of his attempts to talk to her about the town had descended to shouting. But oddly, she seemed less upset about the fact he'd moved to Kilpatrick and reopened the hardware store than the fact he'd agreed to let Roger step in as mayor, after an uncontested election, once his first year was done. But she clearly didn't think Owen was competent enough to run the town either, so how could she be so upset he'd pass on the job?

To make things more complicated, Owen and Sara had been expecting a baby. With Sara's top secret work as a Canadian military intelligence officer, they didn't know how they were ever going to parent their daughter together with them living hours apart.

Then, like a thunderclap, Owen's life as he'd known it had ended.

Sara had been brutally murdered just six weeks after Juniper was born. She'd been shot multiple times and left in her car. The car had been set on fire; Sara's remains had been so badly burned that she had to be identified through dental records.

And now, six months to the day he had lost her, Owen was going to visit her grave.

I miss you, Sara. More than you'll ever know. I need

you and your wisdom down deep in my bones. Even though we had our problems, I don't know how to do all this without you.

If Sara were still alive, she'd know how to save the town. He was sure of it. Yes, they'd fought. He thought she was too single-minded in her focus. She'd been frustrated watching him start things without finishing them and wasn't convinced he was truly dedicated to anything in his life—including her, their daughter or the town. But since she'd been gone, it felt like the tiny pilot light of hope inside his heart had been snuffed out forever.

The town's only traffic light turned red in front of him. He stopped dutifully despite the lack of any cars coming the other way. To his right, a delightful mish-mash of glittery construction paper chains and toddler scribbles filled every corner of the Tatlow's Used Books and Café front window. Travis Tatlow was a retired special victims unit detective with three children under the age of five, a good heart and the ability to not care whether he rubbed any of the town's muckety-mucks the wrong way. Travis's wife, Jess, was one of the most impressive detectives in the OPP. Tonight they were babysitting Owen's daughter, Juniper, for him.

The light turned green, and Owen kept going. He drove up the hill, stopped his snowmobile just inside the gate of the cemetery, dismounted and pulled off his helmet. He'd have reached Sara's graveside faster by going around to the back service road. But he needed the walk to think and to pray. Thick snow swirled down around him, and as he reached up to run a hand through his Kilpatrick-red hair, already he could feel the flakes carpeting his head and clinging to his beard. Inside the hard black storage box mounted on the back of his snowmobile, the bouquet of roses wrapped in cellophane he'd bought to leave at Sara's headstone sat propped against his spare passenger helmet and seemed to have survived the journey with only a minimal amount of petal loss. He took them out, left his own helmet in their place and started walking up the desolate and snowy path through the graves.

Almost immediately, he had the disquieting sense that he wasn't alone.

He stopped and looked back. Long gray shadows spread across the pale snow, stretching out like fingers from between the spruce trees. There was nobody there. Just himself, his thoughts and the dull unending ache in his chest. He turned back and kept walking, listening to the sound of his own feet crunching in the snow. No, he was sure he could hear a second person's too. He stopped walking, but the sound of footsteps continued.

He wasn't alone.

"Hello?" he called. Silence fell. He looked around and saw nothing but snowcapped gravestones and trees. "Is somebody there?"

Nobody answered.

He laid the flowers against Sara's headstone and wiped back the snow, feeling the engraving under his fingertips.

Corporal Marissa "Sara" Jenkins-Kilpatrick.
Canadian Armed Forces.

He knelt in the snow beside her grave and closed his eyes. Sara's face filled his mind, with her determined grin and feisty blue eyes. She'd been the smartest per-

son and strongest woman he'd ever known. Even though
their differences had led to dozens of arguments that
had cut away at the fabric of their relationship, up until
the moment he'd heard of her death, he'd never lost hope
they'd find their way back together. But maybe she had.
After all, although police had found her wallet and cell
phone on her at the time of her death, she hadn't been
wearing her wedding ring.

"Owen?"

He heard his late wife's voice calling his name, softly
and tentatively.

Was he hearing things?

He looked up and there stood Sara, just a few yards
away by the service road, in a long dress and boots, with
wisps of black hair streaming out from under a disheveled bonnet.

A sob caught in his throat as his mind struggled to
understand what his eyes were seeing.

His estranged wife was dead, gone, buried in a coffin in the soil beneath him and was never coming back.
And yet, as Owen pushed himself to his feet, he found
himself saying her name. "Sara? Is that you?"

"Yes!" she replied. He heard fear, joy and relief mingling in her voice. "I'm in trouble and I need your help."

It was impossible. She couldn't be there. She couldn't
be alive. Still, he found himself running toward her, as
something deep inside his heart, far beyond logic, knew
with an unmistakable certainty the woman he'd once
loved and lost was somehow alive and standing there
in the snow in front of him.

But before he could reach her, sudden headlights
pierced the gloom. A dirty white van flew down the ser-

vice road and skidded to a stop between them. He watched as the back door swung open like a gaping mouth, and a man reached out and grabbed Sara around the shoulders and yanked her back, off her feet and into the van.

"Owen!" His name tore like a scream through her lips. "Help me!"

"Sara!" he shouted. Desperately, he ran for her. But he was too late. The door slammed, and the van peeled off into the night.

TWO

Sara's masked attacker shoved her back hard against the cold metal floor of the van. The man crouched over her and waved a gun in her face.

"Stay down!" he bellowed. His loud voice seemed to echo around them. "Don't move or I'll kill you!"

Somehow she knew that no matter what she did now, they weren't planning on letting her out of this alive.

It was the same large man who'd barred Sara's escape when he'd blocked the Zooks' front door earlier that morning. He'd rolled his ski mask up since then so the brim sat just above his eyes like a knit hat and wrapped a thick scarf around the lower half of his face, which she guessed was so he could disguise his features while looking for her without drawing too much attention to himself. His partner, Beau, who'd ransacked the Zooks' kitchen, had done likewise and was now in the driver's seat and speeding down the road as if his own life depended on it.

The men shouted profanities back and forth at each other. Beau wanted his partner, whom he called Coop, to handcuff her. Coop shouted he couldn't do so without

dropping the gun and said she was too scared to do anything. It was clear he thought she wouldn't fight back.
Coop said they'd get out of town, pull over where nobody could hear her scream and "deal with" her there.

The wind howled outside the metal walls of the van,
and the floor shook and rattled beneath her, jolting fresh
pain into her sore and aching body.

She closed her eyes and prayed for a way to escape
them again.

How had they found her? She'd been running from
them all day, for what she guessed had to be fourteen
hours at least. After making her way through the trees
for a while, she'd come out onto a small rural highway shortly after sunrise. A trucker had pulled over to
ask if she needed a ride. She'd turned him down, not
wanting to get into a truck with a stranger but told him
about the home invasion and fire at the Zooks' house
and asked him to call 911 for the fire department and
police, which he did. She'd kept walking, and a while
later a Mennonite family with a horse and buggy had
offered her a ride, which she'd taken to the closest town,
where she'd stopped to rest in an open church. There,
another kind stranger had offered her bus fare for the
next leg of her journey.

But mostly she'd walked and prayed, making her way
to a town she'd known only as a dot on a map, hoping to
find the red-haired man she knew only as Owen. And now,
despite the cold, fear and pain that threatened to overwhelm her, a tiny glimmer of hope flickered in her heart.

She had found Owen, he'd recognized her and he'd
been the same man with kind eyes from her dreams.
Then she'd been abducted before she could reach him

again. The Zooks had gently suggested Owen could be the name of her husband. But she hadn't believed it. Because if he had been, then why had she been wearing the ring on a chain around her neck when she was found instead of on her finger? Why had she been on the run?

Most importantly, if Owen knew who she was and his name was inside her gold ring, why hadn't he been looking for her?

"We're being followed!" Coop snapped.

"By who?" Beau yelled.

"I don't know!" Coop said. "He's on a snowmobile. It's the guy from the grave, I think."

The small flicker of hope grew in her chest. Owen was coming for her.

"I couldn't exactly see what he looked like in the graveyard," Coop added, "and now he's got a helmet on!"

"Well, shoot him!"

"I don't know who he is!" Coop snapped. "You want me to just kill him? You want him dead so badly, you shoot him yourself!"

Slowly, Sara raised herself up to look out the back window. Coop's hand swung, catching her jaw in a backhanded slap and snapping her head sideways.

Pain shot through her skull.

"Stay down!" Coop snarled. "You so much as flinch, and there's more where that came from!"

He stumbled to the back of the van and shoved the door open. Wind and snow rushed inside. She blinked back the tears filling her eyes and saw the helmeted man on a snowmobile. He was still a long way away but coming closer. And while he was just a dark speck against the gray snow, somehow she knew it was Owen.

Prayers filled her heart and mind, asking God to protect him, save his life and keep him safe.

Coop grabbed hold of the top of the door frame with one hand, leaned out and fired. Owen kept coming. The man swore and fired again. The snowmobile swerved. Coop loaded a fresh bullet into the chamber, and his finger brushed the trigger to shoot.

Suddenly a strong, protective impulse burned like a fire through Sara's veins, pushing her through the pain and up to her feet.

He was going to kill Owen unless she stopped him.

She charged across the van at him. A defiant warrior's cry filled her ears, and she realized it was coming from her lips. She grabbed Coop's forearm with both hands, threw her whole weight against it and slammed his hand back against the wall. He bellowed in pain, fought her for the gun and tried to pull it back from her grasp. Vile threats filled her ears. The gun fired wildly past her face. The van swerved. But she didn't let go.

She had to protect Owen. She had to save his life. Regardless of who Owen was to her and what had happened in their past, she couldn't let these criminals kill him now.

Her hands slid to Coop's wrist and twisted with all her might, wrenching the gun from his hand. It fell out the door and into the night. His fist flew toward her face. But before his blow could land, she leaped through the open door and out onto the road below.

Owen watched as Sara tumbled out of the back of the van onto the frozen road in front of him. His golden headlights illuminated her pale and terrified face.

Help me, Lord. I don't have time to stop! I'm going to run right into her.

He squeezed the brakes and swerved hard, both hoping and praying that he wouldn't hit her. The snowmobile skidded off the road, hit a ditch hard and flew up over it and onto the other side. Owen stopped with a jolt, leaped off and turned back to see Sara scrambling down into the ditch after him. He flipped up his visor and ran back for her. The van sped on down the road and disappeared into the distance. Sara stumbled up the other side of the incline toward him, and he reached for her with both hands. Her fingers slid into his.

"Sara," he said. "Is it really you?"

"Yes, I think so," she said. Her voice barely rose above a whisper.

Hang on—had she just said she thought so?

Confusion and wonder filled her face, as if she was as surprised to see him as he was to see her. Her face was pale. Her eyes were hollow with fatigue and ringed with dark circles. Her hair was longer than he'd ever seen it before and fell loose from what looked like an Amish or Mennonite bonnet. For the first time he could remember since their wedding day, she was wearing a dress.

Was she in some kind of disguise?

Had she been on some secret military intelligence operation all this time?

There was no sign of the van now. While he didn't exactly want to stick around and wait to see if it would return, he also didn't want to hop on his snowmobile and take off—either with or without her—before getting some answers.

"I don't really know what's going on," she went on.

"There's a lot to talk about, and I don't even know where to begin explaining. But those men want to kill you. I think they want to kill me too, and they ransacked my friends' home—"

"What friends?" he asked before she could finish. She'd been living with friends? How could she have done this to him? How could she have let him believe she was dead? He pulled his hands from hers and searched her blue eyes for answers. "Sara, where have you been? Tell me what's going on!"

"I honestly don't know," she started. "I don't remember anything—"

But the roar of a van's engine filled the air before she could explain any further. He looked up. The kidnappers were on their way back.

"Come on." He ran for the snowmobile. "We'll talk later." And boy did they have a lot to talk about. "Right now, we've got to get out of here."

He pulled the second helmet out and handed it to her. She slid it on, and he hesitated. Normally he'd have jumped on the front, and she'd have gotten on the back. But between her slight frame and the custom seat he'd installed, it was technically possible for her to sit in front of him and for him to reach around her. It would be a lot trickier and his steering would suffer. But he wouldn't have to worry about her falling off at every bump or someone shooting her in the back. Despite everything that had happened, something deep inside him still needed to hold and protect her.

Tires screeched as the van came to a stop. Gunfire shook the air. The men hadn't even waited to get close before they'd started shooting.

"Get on," he said. "Slide all the way to the front. I'm going to sit behind you and drive. You're going to be between my arms."

She jumped on without arguing, and that was the moment he knew for certain that something had changed since he'd seen her last. The Sara he'd loved and lost would've argued with him. She might've even insisted she drive.

A chill of fear ran down his spine that was deeper than his fear of the men firing at them and the immediate danger they were in. What had happened to Sara in the six months since he'd seen her last? Why was she different? Why were people trying to kill them? Where had she been?

And why had she come back now?

There was no time to ask her or even pause to think. All he could do was jump on the back, rev the engine and drive. They flew across the snow as the sound of gunshots and shouting came from behind them. Then he heard the van engine roar again. Owen cut straight across the field. The snowmobile bounced across the uneven ground. It would be enough to give him a head start, but all he was doing was cutting across a large square. The van would still be able to drive around the outside and catch up to them. After that, he could play cat and mouse for a while, especially once he made it to the forest line and slipped between the trees. But the van was faster; he wouldn't be able to evade it forever, and he only had fifteen minutes left of gas.

"We need to find a place to hide!" Owen shouted. "How long have they been after you?"

"All day," Sara said, though he could barely hear her voice in the wind. "They broke in before I woke up."

All day? Sunrise had been over fourteen hours ago.

"Where's your vehicle?" he asked.

"I don't have one," she said. "I'm on foot."

She'd been outrunning these men on foot that long? He could feel her back pressed up against his chest and her arms resting just inside of his. Questions welled up inside him like competing waves crashing on the shore. Who was the person Owen had laid to rest in her grave? How could she have let him believe she was dead? What kind of woman would do such a thing? How could he ever begin to understand, let alone forgive her? How could he feel so angry, so betrayed and yet so relieved to hold her at the same time?

A paraphrase of Jesus's words in the parable of the prodigal son rushed unbidden to his mind. *Be merry, for she was dead and is alive again. She was lost and now is found.*

Then it hit him with a start—Sara hadn't asked once about their baby daughter.

What did that mean?

He needed help.

"I'm calling a friend!" he shouted. "We can't run forever, so unless you've got a better idea, I'm taking us somewhere we can hide."

The edge of the field loomed ahead of him. He'd have to turn onto the road when he reached it, unless he wanted to crash into the river ahead. The van was now rounding the corner to his left. In a few moments, the kidnappers would be right back on his tail again and in range to fire.

"Call Travis!" he ordered the hands-free phone connection inside his helmet. Almost immediately, he heard ringing in his ears. Then he heard a tired and familiar-sounding voice.

"Yo, Owen!" Travis said. "Just got your little one down to sleep along with my older two. Juniper is a sweetie. My new little one, on the other hand, is the only holdout."

Travis and Jess's baby girl, Lottie, had been born just three weeks earlier, adding a third to the two other little ones they'd adopted when friends of Travis's had tragically died. It was a full house, and for now Jess was home on maternity leave.

"I've got a…situation!" Owen shouted and then realized he had no clue how to describe what was happening.

"Where are you?" Travis asked. The former detective's voice was suddenly all business. It helped Owen focus.

"On Rural Lane Three, heading east," Owen said.

"On snowmobile?" Travis confirmed.

He'd left his truck at the Tatlows when he'd dropped off Juniper and ridden his snowmobile from there.

"Yup," Owen said.

"What's happening?"

"Two armed and unknown men on my tail, in a van. They've been shooting, and I won't be able to outrun them forever."

"You injured?" Travis asked, and Owen was thankful his friend was asking about basic details rather than why this was happening.

"No," Owen said.

"I take it they know who you are?" Travis asked.

Owen wasn't sure.

"Sara," he called. "Do they know who I am?"

"No!" she shouted. "They said they didn't recognize you."

"Who are you with?" Travis asked.

"I'm with—" Owen started but the words froze on his tongue. *I'm with Sara and she's not dead.* "I'm with a woman. They kidnapped her but she escaped. Apparently they've been chasing her for over twelve hours, mostly on foot." He heard Travis blow out a hard breath. "Look, it's really complicated, and they might be after her because of a secret military operation, but she's not telling me anything, so I don't really know."

"Gotcha," Travis said, sounding like he was processing this much quicker than Owen possibly could. "Then my guess is they're not about to give up easy. Is this a woman you know personally? Is she connected to you?"

How on earth could he answer that?

"She's very connected to me," Owen said. "She's my…" *Estranged wife, who worked in military intelligence, had my child, then disappeared, faked her death and lied to me?* "She's basically family."

"All right," Travis said, "my biggest concern right now is getting you here while making sure they can't track you and don't know you're here." Owen heard him call to Jess and brief her quickly. He couldn't make out what Jess said in return. Then Travis was back. "How attached are you to your snowmobile?"

The one Owen had lovingly restored and custom-built over years?

"Not as attached as I am to my actual life," Owen said. He glanced in the rearview mirror. The van was right on his tail. Large rock formations loomed ahead. He turned hard to the right, off the road and onto a path between the trees. The van swerved along the road after them until they were almost parallel.

Travis outlined in short and crisp detail exactly what route he wanted Owen to take to his and Jess's farmhouse and where to ditch the snowmobile.

"We've got state-of-the-art surveillance cameras hidden all around this place," Travis added. "Nobody's setting foot on this property without us knowing, let alone breaching the house. The falling snow will hide your tracks. They won't find you, and you'll be safe here until we figure all this out. Just get here in one piece. We'll be praying."

Owen thanked his friend and ended the call. Then for several long, agonizing moments, there was nothing to do but drive. He weaved through town, doubling back, cutting down alleys and taking sharp corners, as if the small town of Kilpatrick was his own little obstacle course. Then the buildings were behind him and he was out in the countryside again. At times he'd lose sight of the van for a few minutes, only to see its headlights again looming between the trees. Finally he drove up a long hill, praying with each breath the engine wouldn't give out, and then down again as fast as he could, whizzing through the forest and swerving around trees. The lights of the Tatlow farm flickered ahead. He saw a pond spreading out in a pale sheet of ice between the trees. He steered toward it.

"On the count of three, we jump off into the snowbank on our right," he said. "Got it?"

"Got it!" Sara called.

He steered the snowmobile straight and prayed to God for help. A snowbank rose ahead to his right.

"One!" he shouted. "Two. Three!"

He let go of the handles, wrapped his arms tightly around his estranged wife and jumped. They leaped together. For a moment, their bodies tumbled and rolled in the snow. He pulled away and sat up. He watched his custom-built snowmobile glide smoothly across the ice for one majestic moment, then he heard the ice groan, followed by the sharp sound of it cracking open, and watched as it swallowed his vehicle whole. The snowmobile sank into the lake and was gone.

"Well, now they won't be able to find us by looking for the snowmobile," he said. "I couldn't risk hiding it in a barn somewhere, knowing we're up against people who're relentless enough to spend a day tracking you across the province. The snow is already covering our tracks. They won't know we're here." He blew out a hard breath. "How many months did it even take me to build that thing?"

"I don't remember..." she started.

His question had been rhetorical, but he was getting tired of hearing her say that.

"We were living in Ottawa," he said, "in that place on Woodroff, and you told me I'd never finish it."

"Owen." Her voice rose sharply. She grabbed his hand. "Listen to me—when I say I don't remember, I mean it. I was shot in the head. I was injured. My memory is gone. I don't know who you are, who I am, or anything about my life or what happened to me before the Zooks rescued me six months ago."

His heart froze midbeat, and his mind struggled to

process what she was saying. Sara had amnesia? He opened his mouth, but no words came out. Instead, his gaze moved away from her face, through the trees to the Tatlow farmhouse, where their daughter slept.

No wonder she hadn't asked about Juniper.

Sara didn't know she had a child.

THREE

"Where are we?" Sara asked. Through the trees, she could see the lights of a three-story farmhouse with a wide front porch. "Is this your home?"

"No, this is my friend's house. I still live in the apartment above the hardware store," he said. "Not that you'd remember that. I'm also still the town's mayor."

He sounded confused. No, more than that. Owen sounded angry.

"What I don't understand," Owen added, "is if you don't remember me, what are you even doing here? Why did you come to the graveyard? Why did you approach me and call my name?"

Sara was still half crouched beside him in the snowbank. Even though she had no memory of the snowmobile that he'd just sunk into a pond, it was clear from his tone of voice that he felt he had no choice but to sink it and that it pained him to lose it. It was also clear he knew exactly who she was and was really conflicted about seeing her again.

"I was in the graveyard because when the fireworks started going off, I saw the church," she said. "And the

Zooks told me that if I was ever in trouble, I should head for a church. I'm in Kilpatrick because of this—"

Sara's fingers reached into her collar, felt for her golden chain and pulled out the ring. Her fingers ran over the familiar metal that she'd held on to for months as the only link to her former identity and life.

"I was found with this ring on a chain around my neck," Sara said. "It was the only personal belonging I had on me when I was found, except for my clothes. It says Sara Owen Kilpatrick."

"So that's where it was," he said, almost to himself. "And here I just assumed you'd gotten rid of it."

He suddenly sounded very weary, like he'd been running for days and the fatigue had just caught up with him.

"What?" she asked. "You thought I'd gotten rid of the ring? Why?"

He paused for a long moment as if trying to figure out what to say. Then he pulled himself to his feet and sighed.

"Honestly, it's an incredibly long story, and I don't even know where to start," he said. "Or, to be honest, how much I even believe any of the thoughts going through my head right now. Let's just get inside, get warmed up and then we can start to untangle whatever this is."

Okay. She respected that. But there was still one question that burned at the back of her mind that she hesitated to ask—but desperately needed to know.

"But is this a wedding ring?" she asked. "Are we husband and wife?"

Owen didn't answer. Instead, a long silence stretched

between them, punctuated only by the howl of the wind and the rustle of the leaves as he stood and stared out at the horizon. Then he said, quietly, "Yes, Sara. We were still married."

"Were," she repeated. So they weren't anymore? "What happened to us?"

But instead of answering her question, he ran his hand over his face.

"We were legally separated," he said. "I guess this means we still are."

"What?" Before she could even begin to ask him what he meant, they saw headlights cutting through the trees and heard the sound of a vehicle approaching. Owen held his hand to his lips, signaling her to be quiet. Seconds later the kidnappers' white van drove through the trees and up the long driveway. She ducked behind a tree, her heart pounding hard in her chest. Then she felt Owen move beside her. His hand brushed the small of her back, and there was something both comforting and familiar about it.

"They've found us," she whispered.

"Not necessarily." Owen's voice was soft and protective in her ear. "Hopefully they lost our trail and are now just searching house to house."

They watched as the vehicle rolled to a stop in front of the farmhouse. The van doors opened. But even as her two kidnappers climbed out, a tall man with broad shoulders and a determined gait strode out of the house and onto the front porch.

"I'm Travis Tatlow!" he called. Authority rang in his voice. "This is my home. How can I help you gentlemen?"

"We're looking for a girl," Coop said. His chest puffed

out with a bravado Sara suspected he thought was intimidating. "Came by this way with a guy on a snowmobile. You happen to see them?"

"Gosh, I hate to hear about a woman being in trouble," Travis said. He shook his head. "Sorry, only woman in the house is my wife."

"Can we come in and look around?" Beau asked. There was something in his tone that more than implied he was giving Travis a choice between doing things the easy way or facing some unwanted consequences. Beau pulled a gun from inside his jacket and held it casually at his side as if it were a softball he was debating whether to throw. As if on cue, Coop pulled out a weapon too. She couldn't tell if it was the same gun she'd kicked out of the van or if they'd had extra firepower on them. "Just give us a few minutes and then we'll be out of your hair."

"Hey, honey!" Travis yelled toward the house over his shoulder. "Got a sec? There are two men with guns here wanting to come in and look around!" He turned back to the men. "My wife's a senior detective, actually, with the Ontario Provincial Police. She specializes in all kinds of missing-person cases. I'd be happy to put your guns in our weapons safe for you, if you'd like to come inside for a cup of tea. I'll put on the kettle, and I'm sure she'd be more than happy to take your statement and provide you any assistance you need."

Sara's kidnappers hesitated.

Travis then chuckled, almost apologetically.

"Actually guys, I hate to mention it, but to be honest I can barely see your faces with you all bundled up like that," he added. "Can you at least pull down your scarves a bit more so I can better see who I'm talking to?"

The tone was light. But somehow, it also wasn't a suggestion. Travis took a step farther into the light. His heavy winter coat lay open, and as he moved, Sara caught a glimpse of the tiny bundle strapped to his chest.

It looked like he was wearing a tiny baby in a chest harness.

Suddenly, the memory of a baby crying in her nightmares filled her mind. Fear gripped her chest, choking her breath from her lungs.

"We have to stop him," Sara said. She turned to Owen. "He's got a baby, and we can't let those criminals in his house or anywhere near his family."

"It's okay," Owen said. "Trust me. Travis has a plan, and it doesn't involve letting them anywhere near his house or his family."

But his voice didn't sound as confident as she'd have liked it to. The two men hesitated a moment, then turned around and headed back for their van.

"No?" Travis called after them. Their doors slammed. Then the engine roared. "If you guys can't find her, how about you swing back with some flyers? I'd be happy to put them up around town. And like I said, my wife's more than happy to do the full police thing."

The van pulled out of the driveway before Travis could offer her kidnappers any more assistance. Travis stood and watched them go. The sound of the engine disappeared into the distance. Owen let out a long breath.

"This is good," Owen said, like he was trying to convince himself along with her. "The fact Travis stood his ground and showed them he can't be intimidated will deter them from coming round here again on a fishing expedition. They probably won't bother with the Tatlows again unless they're certain they have something to do with you, which we'll have to make sure doesn't happen. But more importantly, Travis probably also got some good footage of them on his hidden security cameras. I expect he was hoping to keep them there long enough for Jess to run facial recognition and see if there were any outstanding warrants she could call in to her colleagues. Even with a partial, it can be pretty accurate. Not that I need to explain spycraft or subterfuge to you."

What? Again, nothing he said answered any of the pressing questions on her mind. Like if he'd known she was missing, why hadn't he at least filed a police report? Especially considering she'd been shot.

Something inside her wanted to argue with him. But she wasn't even sure why or what about. It was like there was a scrap of a song playing in the back of her head, and not only was she struggling to remember its tune, but she knew she used to sing the harmony.

"All clear!" Travis shouted loudly in their direction. "They're off the property and, by the look of things, are headed to check the next farm."

"Thanks!" Owen called back. Then he turned to Sara. "Come on, let's get inside. I don't know about you, but I'm freezing."

She'd been outside a whole lot longer than he'd been and had reached the point where she was beyond feeling cold and tired, and instead just felt numb. But she knew the adrenaline she was running on would burn out eventually, and the full strain of everything her body and mind had gone through would hit her like a freight train.

They jogged through the trees toward the house. She

noticed Owen had reached for her hand but then stopped short of taking it. Travis met them on the porch and held the door open.

"Come on in," he said, "and welcome. I'm Travis."

"I'm Sara," she said.

"Nice to meet you." Travis waited until they were inside then closed the door and locked it, with both the knob lock and a dead bolt. They stepped into a large warm room, where children's toys spilled out from every nook and cranny. A tiny baby squirmed in a bassinet beside a roaring fire.

Sara blinked at the baby and did a double take at Travis. That was when she realized what she'd thought was a child tucked close to Travis's chest was actually just a life-size plastic doll. Travis reached in, pulled the doll out and tossed it onto a chair. Owen exhaled sharply, and she knew he'd thought so too.

Travis quirked an eyebrow at Owen.

"You thought I actually went out there to face whoever's after this poor woman with my three-week-old daughter on my chest?" he asked. Travis sounded far more bemused than offended.

"Yes," Owen admitted.

"Huh," Travis said. He took the harness off, dropped it on the chair beside the door and reached for his little girl. The baby looked so tiny inside his large hands, and Sara felt some unknown thing twist inside her heart. "Good. Then I must've really fooled them. We want them to think we've got nothing to hide here, along with suspecting we're too much trouble to bother with. Now, by the sound of things, you've got some doozy of a story for me."

Travis cradled his daughter to his chest. "All the other kids are upstairs," he added, with a glance at Owen that spoke volumes Sara couldn't decipher. "You mentioned you two are 'very connected' and 'basically family'. So, am I right in assuming that she already knows about the kid situation?"

"No, she does not," Owen said evenly. "No idea at all about it."

"Ah," Travis said. The indecipherable look deepened.

Okay, now what did that mean?

"What kid situation?" she asked. But neither man answered her.

"Jess ran the license plates and the faces," Travis went on, "and will alert her colleagues to get a warrant out just as soon as you let us know what we're dealing with."

"So your wife really is a cop?" Sara asked.

"Oh absolutely," Travis said, pride filling his face. "She's on maternity leave for a few more weeks. But she's definitely a detective, and one of the absolute best."

"Thanks, honey." A woman's voice came from beyond a doorway to her right. "But sadly, the license plates were fakes, and we've got no matches on the faces so far."

Sara turned. A petite and pretty woman with blond hair in a loose bun walked in from the kitchen. She wiped her hands on a paint-stained pink apron.

"But we'll keep looking," the woman said. "I'm Jess. I see you've met Travis and our baby, Lottie. Do you want to sit? Or maybe lie down? I can help you out of your wet clothes and get you something to eat." Her tone was gentle and understanding. Sara was clearly not the first vulnerable person in danger whom Jess had dealt with. "I get that it can be scary trusting anyone after you've been through something tough, so take all the time you need to get yourself turned around and to fill us in. You'll be safe here."

"Thank you," Sara said. "I appreciate it. I'm sort of beyond feeling hungry right now, but I'm sure that'll change once my adrenaline slows down." The men had taken off their winter gear. But Sara was still dressed in her coat, bonnet, gloves and boots. Right now, she felt like if she so much as bent down to untie her laces, she'd collapse. "I'm Sara."

Jess's eyes widened.

"You're Sara?" Jess repeated. In all the chaos, Sara hadn't had time to question Owen about their marriage and didn't want to do it now in front of strangers. But she wondered what Jess and Travis knew about her that she didn't. "And you're also Amish?"

Jess turned to look at Travis, and the couple shared a long and inscrutable look.

"Yes, I'm *plain*," Sara said. "That's what we call people who live by the *Ordnung*. For the past six months, I've been living with an elderly couple named Petrus and Hadassah Zook. Right now they're traveling to visit family in Pennsylvania Dutch Country and left me home alone. Today, just before sunrise, those same two men burst in and ransacked the house. They were looking for something, but I don't know what. They tried to kidnap me, and then burned the farmhouse down. They called each other Beau and Coop, if that helps."

"It might," Jess said.

"Sara's been on the run ever since," Owen said. "A lot of it on foot."

"So, these two guys have been tracking her all day?" Travis asked.

"Yup," Owen said.

The color drained from Travis's face, then he sat, as if the blood had also drained from his limbs. Something about seeing the former detective look so rattled made the fear tighten inside Sara's chest.

"Okay," Travis said. "So this is even bigger than I thought."

Sara watched as the three of them shared a glance, as if they all knew something she didn't. She didn't like it.

"Look, I don't actually remember anything about myself or my life before six months ago," Sara said. "I was shot in the head, just a graze thankfully, but got a really bad concussion and amnesia."

Travis looked at Owen. Jess shot them both a glare as if warning them to watch what they said, but there was something protective about it that made Sara feel safe.

"Petrus found me in a river in Ontario Amish country six months ago," Sara went on. "He thought I was dead at first. He carried me home in his buggy to his wife, Hadassah, then called his brother, who's a doctor. Dr. Amos said I'd been grazed by a bullet and had a concussion. He called the police, but there weren't any missing people matching my description. It was weeks before the headaches died down enough that I could even walk. The Zooks left two days ago to visit family in Pennsylvania. Hadassah's brother was dying, and they thought it was their last chance to see him."

Owen nodded as if he understood.

"And of course no passport or ID meant you couldn't go with them," Owen murmured.

"Exactly," she said, "and I didn't want them putting their lives on hold for me."

She blew out a long breath and realized she didn't want these people to do that either. "You know the rest. Beau and Coop broke in today, tossed the place, set the house on fire and came after me."

It was possible the fire wasn't intentional, she realized, considering the house had several oil lamps they might've tried to light. Had the house burned down? Or had the snow put it out before the entire Zook's farmhouse was engulfed?

She filled them in on the rest of her journey, from how a trucker had helped her call it in to police to how she'd made it all the way to Kilpatrick. The others listened.

"Have you been anywhere but their home in the past six months?" Travis asked.

"Only visiting other families in town and the local meeting house," Sara said. "We went to an *Englischer* holiday market in a nearby town in December."

"Maybe that's where whoever is after you noticed you," Travis said. "Amish villages won't have security cameras, but a regular town might."

"Does your Amish family know where you are now?" Jess asked.

"No," Sara said. "The Amish don't have home phones. Only a communal shared phone in town. Petrus and Hadassah won't arrive at their destination for at least two days. And I didn't want to pause long enough to try to get through to Petrus's brother, Dr. Amos. It's hard to contact someone securely through a communal phone. You don't know who'll answer or who will overhear." It would also be incredibly easy to bug. Not that Sara had any idea how she knew that. "The doctor and his wife have five kids and three grandkids, and I didn't want whoever was after me to come after them."

"Probably wise," Jess said, "for now."

"Plus, who knows who we can trust," Owen said.

What did he mean by that?

"I'm confident that nobody in the Amish community had anything to do with this," Sara said sharply.

"Yeah, I mean sure," Owen said, "but that doesn't mean they won't accidentally tell someone who you are."

A long moment of silence fell around the room, which seemed to hang thick with unspoken thoughts. Finally, it was Jess who broke the silence, with a hesitancy that made Sara think Jess suspected she already knew the answer. "And why did you come here?"

Sara pressed her lips together, and before she could answer, Owen did.

"Because as you've might've guessed, this is my Sara," Owen said. "My estranged wife Sara. She had her wedding ring on her. It had the words *Sara Owen Kilpatrick* engraved in it."

"Wow." Travis ran his hand over the back of his head. "And she doesn't know anything about…anything?" His voice trailed off as if he caught himself before saying anything more, but she couldn't help but notice as his eyes darted up toward the second floor.

"Look, clearly you all know something about me that I don't," Sara said. "It's like you're all dancing around it, and I'm sure you have your reasons. I'm exhausted and terrified, but despite what you might think, I'm not fragile. So I'd really appreciate it if you were all straight with me."

"For what it's worth," Owen said, "I've never thought you were fragile."

Jess looked at Travis, and he nodded.

"I'm going to put Lottie in her crib and call Anne," Jess said. She reached for the sleeping baby. Travis handed Lottie to her, and Jess cradled her in her arms.

"I'll go with you," Travis said and stood quickly.

"Anne is a doctor and a concussion specialist," Jess added. "She also helped out with an important witness-protection case a few Christmases ago and housed a witness with a concussion for us. You can trust her. She's the best doctor I know. She's also experienced in helping people hide and stay off the grid. That case she helped us with involved a woman in the military."

Jess and Travis disappeared down the hall. Sara turned toward Owen so sharply she felt the twinge of a headache form at the back of her neck.

"Why does it matter that this doctor has worked with someone in the military?" Sara asked. "Was I a soldier?"

No, it couldn't be true. She lived a *plain* and pacifist life. She loved the peacefulness of it, along with the sense of family and community. She used to wield a weapon for a living? Is that why she hadn't been afraid to jump out a window or disarm Coop?

"You were in military intelligence," Owen said.

Sara's legs felt wobbly. The ache grew stronger, and her head began to spin.

"Is that why you didn't come looking for me?" she asked. "I don't understand. Why wasn't I listed as missing? Why is everyone so surprised to see me now?"

Owen's hand brushed her arm.

"We thought you were dead," he said. "A dead body was found in your car, with your wallet and phone. It was badly burned in a fire, but that body was forensically identified as you. When you found me, I was visiting your grave."

Dead? Sudden nausea swept over her, as strongly and severely as it had in the early days of the concussion. The sound of her pulse filled her ears.

Her legs gave way, and she felt herself collapse.

Owen reached out and caught Sara in his arms before she hit the floor.

"Easy now," he said. "It's going to be okay."

He lowered her gently into a chair and then knelt beside her. His hand brushed the side of her face, and Sara's blue eyes fluttered open.

"I'm fine," she said firmly. A glimmer of defiance flashed in the golden specks of her irises. "I'm just tired and overwhelmed. That's all."

He felt a sad chuckle build at the back of his throat but caught it before it escaped his lips. Yeah, that was 100 percent Sara. Stubborn and determined. Always insisting that she was all right when she clearly wasn't and that she didn't need help when she obviously did. It was something he'd admired so much while also been incredibly irritated by at times. Seemed some parts of the woman he'd loved were still in there. Even if they were the qualities that had driven them apart.

And here he was, still down on one knee beside her chair. They were eye level. So close that all it would take was for him to lean forward slightly to brush his lips against her cheeks and kiss away the tears, fatigue and pain he could see floating in her eyes. He'd been through so much in the past few months. It had all left him too tired for words. Now here he was, face-to-face with someone whose eyes were filled with the same exhaustion and confusion he was sure were mirrored in his. Sara might be the only person who could actually understand what he'd gone through and who felt the same.

He swallowed hard.

"You were an intelligence officer in Ottawa," he said. "I couldn't figure out what I wanted to do with my life. When my cousin died in a car crash, I moved here, took over the hardware store and stepped in as mayor. You stayed behind. We were separated when you died. Well, when I thought you died. We'd been married for two years, but our marriage fell apart because we wanted different things. It may not sound like much of a reason, and it's a much longer and more complicated story than that. But in a nutshell, that's what it came down to."

She blinked. Her eyes met his, and he held her gaze.

There was more, so much more. They had a precious baby daughter asleep upstairs. She wouldn't stay asleep forever. He needed to tell Sara about her. But somehow his mouth couldn't find the words.

How did he just come out and tell her she had a six-month-old baby she'd forgotten?

"I know you don't have a good reason to trust me," he added. "But the Sara I knew always had great instincts about people. It was one of your gifts and what made you an excellent officer. So you should know somehow in your gut that I'd never hurt you and will do every-thing in my power to protect you."

And I can't wait to reintroduce you to our baby.

"I know," she said softly. "I keep seeing your face in my dreams, and it always makes me feel safe."

Something sharp pricked in his chest. It reminded him of how he'd felt years ago, the moment he'd first realized his heart would break if he lost her.

"I can remember my childhood," she said. "More or less. And my life into my teenage years. I know I was an only child and my parents are dead. But I don't have any memories of you. How long have we known each other?"

"Three years," he said.

"Huh," she said and tilted her head to the side. "And we were married for two?"

"It was a whirlwind romance," he said.

He'd spent countless nights lying awake wondering if maybe that was why things had failed. They'd gotten married too fast. They hadn't known each other well enough. He'd never been good at making decisions, but she'd seemed so certain they were right for each other, and he'd been so deeply in love.

Sara slowly eased her hands out of her gloves. Her fingers were so stiff and bright red from the cold, he could see she struggled to bend them.

"Your hands look frozen," he said. "Are they cold?"

"Actually, they feel like they're on fire."

"Here. Let me help you."

He held out his hands to her, palms up. She rested her hands on his. They were ice-cold. For a long moment they stayed there, with his palms radiating heat into hers. His thumb brushed the side of her hand and she winced.

"Still burns?" he asked.

"Yeah," she said. "They're stiff. They're so stiff I can barely bend them."

"Can I help you out of your boots?" he asked.

She hesitated a long moment, then nodded. "Please," she said. "After all, I don't want to track snow all over these nice people's floor."

He eased her hands away from his, reached for a soft blanket that was lying over the chair Travis had vacated and wrapped it around her hands. Then he steadied himself on one knee. She braced her right foot against the other one and pulled back the hem of her skirt so he could see the laces of her boots. He started to untie them slowly, battling with the knots. He finished loosening her right boot enough that he could ease it off her foot. She was wearing thick wool socks underneath, along with a pair of leggings as thick as long johns. At his request, she pressed her foot into his hand, wincing as pins and needles shot through it. He reached for the other boot.

"Thankfully, it doesn't look like you have hypothermia," Owen said. She silently thanked God for that too. "But I'm glad Jess called a real doctor to see you."

Her back stiffened.

"Petrus's brother, Dr. Amos, is a real doctor," she said sharply.

"But he's Amish."

"Yes, but that doesn't mean he doesn't have a medical license same as any other doctor and that he can't diagnose a concussion," Sara said.

Owen frowned.

"Do you think the Amish are uneducated?" she pressed.

"I don't know what I think of the Amish," Owen said. "I've never met any."

Did she really want to argue about this?

"Well, then trust me when I tell you that they did everything they could to help me," Sara said. "You don't believe me?"

"You used to work in military intelligence," he pointed out. "The Amish don't even use electricity or computers."

She didn't answer, and for a long moment neither of them said anything. He focused on battling the frozen knots in her laces.

"Anyway, Dr. Amos said my memories might come back over time," she said finally. "Rest might help. So might familiar sounds and sights."

"Is there anything else that comes to you in your dreams?" he asked.

"I remember running and falling," she said. "There's this sound of roaring. I remember a hospital bed and a baby crying." He tugged her other boot off so quickly he fell back on his heels. "Then I saw you. Dr. Amos thinks the images are out of order, based on emotions, not history."

Footsteps creaked in the hallway behind them. Owen leaped to his feet and turned. Jess and Travis had reappeared in the hallway.

"Hey," Owen said. He ran both his hands down his legs. "I was just helping Sara take her gloves and boots off."

"Lottie is asleep in her crib, finally," Jess said, "and I got through to Anne. I told her Sara was on the run, so she's also bringing some clothes for you."

"Owen told me you all thought I was dead," Sara said.

Jess turned and her hands snapped to her hips as she glanced from Owen to Travis.

"Anne said the best thing we can do right now is keep Sara calm," Jess said. "Because the combination of extreme physical and emotional stress could worsen the effects of the concussion, set back her recovery and make everything worse. So let's put any more upsetting revelations on hold for now until Sara's managed to recover a bit from her ordeal today. There will be plenty of time to go over everything later. Just throwing bombshells at a person willy-nilly is the worst thing we can do right now."

In other words, no telling Sara about the tiny baby girl asleep in a crib on the second floor.

"Anne's on her way and should be here in an hour," Jess added. "Thankfully, her eldest son is home from college and able to take care of her youngest. Until then, I suggest Sara get warmed up, have a bite to eat and rest if she can."

She reached for Sara's arm and helped her up to her feet.

"Don't get me wrong," Jess told Sara. Her voice was softer this time. "I fully agree we need to tackle this thing head-on and from multiple angles. But first things first—we need to make sure you're okay."

Jess and Sara headed across the room and down the hallway. A door closed. Owen sat down hard in the chair

Sara had just vacated, feeling like a balloon that some-one had recently popped. Travis dropped into a chair opposite him.

"So, how are you?" Travis asked.

"Are you asking as a friend or a former special vic-tims unit detective?" Owen asked.

"Both."

Owen smiled wearily. "I don't know how I'm feeling. I'm numb."

Wordlessly, Travis got up and walked into the kitchen. A moment later, he was back with a mug of green liquid he pushed into Owen's hands. It was hot.

"It's peppermint tea with four sugars," Travis said. "It's sweet and it'll help with the shock you must be feeling. I'd offer you something with caffeine, but sadly caffeine and I don't mix."

Owen remembered that when Travis was a cop, he'd pushed himself so hard he'd gotten addicted to energy drinks. He took a deep gulp and grimaced. "It tastes like liquid candy cane."

"Well, when you're done with that, I've got one that tastes like hot gingerbread soup," Travis said. "I got a lot of misguided seasonal herbal teas over the holidays. Now, does Sara have any relatives we need to think about contacting?"

"No," Owen said. "We bonded over the fact we're both only children and lost our parents in our early twen-ties."

Owen took another sip of the molten peppermint and winced.

"Normal relationship?"

"I guess so," Owen said. "We bickered a lot. We're very different people."

"No possessive exes or violent rivals in the picture?" Travis asked.

"No," Owen said. "We fell apart all by ourselves in very boring and tedious ways."

The floorboards creaked, and they looked up to see Jess walking back into the room. She perched on the arm of her husband's chair and looped her fingers through his.

"Sara's getting changed," she said. "I'll set up the bedroom in the attic for her tonight. In the meantime, she's in my office. I don't recommend any of you go back to your apartment above the store tonight."

For the first time since the night had started, Owen looked at the clock. It had been about nine when he'd left to take the flowers to the graveside. Now it was almost midnight.

Travis looked up at her. "Do you need us to backtrack?"

"No, I think I got the gist of it as I came in," Jess said. "Normal marriage, boring fights, no obvious suspects from her personal life. Any problem with her career?"

Now he really felt like he was being grilled, and by two detectives.

"Besides the fact she worked in military intelligence and couldn't tell me what she was working on?" Owen asked rhetorically. "All I know is she turned down some assignments."

"What do you remember about the day of her death?" Jess pressed.

"I'd moved up to Kilpatrick some weeks earlier,"

Owen said, "but she'd never been up here. I always drove down to Ottawa to see Juniper. Sara just showed up at the hardware store out of the blue, told me we needed to talk but that first she needed to do something, and asked me to watch the baby. I remember Juniper was asleep in her car seat, wrapped up in a little baby quilt that Sara had been sewing for her. She handed me the baby and the diaper bag and left. I never saw her again."

Travis dropped Jess's hand and leaned forward, his elbows resting on his knees. "She didn't say who she was meeting?"

"No."

"Did you believe her?" Jess asked.

"At first," Owen said. "But when she didn't come back, I thought she'd just abandoned the baby. The next day police showed up at my door and told me her body had been found."

"Only it wasn't her body," Travis said. "Did they do a DNA test?"

"No," Owen said. "They identified her by dental records. It was quicker."

Jess stood back up and started to pace.

"So, we have someone working in military intelligence who was estranged from her husband and had a newborn baby," Jess said. "Her death was so elaborately faked it had to involve considerable planning. We can't rule out that Sara herself was involved in it."

Owen blinked. "You suspect Sara was involved in something criminal?"

"We can't rule it out," Jess said.

"She might've faked her own death," Travis said, "or

killed the woman now buried in her grave. Sara might not be dead, but another woman is and that woman's family probably has no idea what happened to her. In the meantime, I suggest that Sara stays here."

"No, I'm not staying." Sara's voice sounded from the hall. "I'm leaving."

Owen leaped to his feet. Sara was standing in the doorway. She'd changed into long, flowing gray pants and a white tunic that almost brushed her knees. Her dark hair was wet and fell loose to her shoulders.

"How long have you been listening?" Owen asked.

What had she overheard?

Sara's chin rose. "Enough to know that you all think I might be a criminal, who faked her own death and killed someone."

Owen exhaled. So she hadn't overheard the earlier bit about her baby.

"Nobody said that—" Owen started.

"Actually, I did," Travis cut him off. "But it was merely a hypothetical, and you can't blame Owen for something I said."

"But he didn't jump to defend me either," Sara said. "I shouldn't have come here. I should've gone straight to the police—"

"I am police," Jess interjected. Her tone was firm but not unkind. "And considering the magnitude of this crime, we can't rule out the possibility that some form of corrupt law enforcement was involved. We can help you."

"You have kids," Sara said, and her voice rose. "And I don't want to bring danger into your lives. I've just discovered that one woman is already dead because of me. I don't want to get anybody else hurt or put any of you in danger."

The sweet and plaintive sound of a baby's cry cut the air. Their daughter, little Juniper, was crying out as if she heard her mother's voice and was calling to her.

Sara's eyes widened, and her hand rose to her lips as if somehow she knew it too. "That's my baby!"

FOUR

Sara leaped from her chair and ran blindly down the hallway toward the sound of her baby crying. Walls of colorful children's art and smiling family portraits blurred as she passed them. Behind her, she could hear Owen calling to her. But his voice seemed almost muffled and on the edge of her brain. All she could hear was her baby. She reached a staircase and ran up it, taking the stairs two at a time. She came out into another hallway, this one narrower. Doors surrounded her on either side. She paused. The baby's voice seemed to come from all directions at once, and the walls were closing in around her.

"Sara," Owen said. "Wait. It's okay. I'll take you to her."

He wasn't shouting, she realized, or trying to stop her. Rather, his voice was gentle and soft. Urgent, yes. But also filled with regret.

Then she felt his warm hand touch her shoulder and she realized he'd reached her. He guided her down the hallway and wordlessly opened a door to her right. Heart pounding, she stepped through the doorway and met her daughter's eyes.

The baby was standing in the crib in a yellow one-sie. Her chubby fingers gripped the railing. Her tears stopped, and her little eyes widened. A sob choked in Sara's throat. Her daughter was tiny and perfect. She guessed between seven and eight months old, with wide blue eyes, a rosebud mouth and a light brush of red hair on top of her head.

Her mother's eyes and her father's hair.

Silently, the baby stared at her. Then her fingers slipped from the railing, and she fell back onto her bottom. Her little mouth opened to wail, but before the tears could fall, Sara rushed across the room, swept the little girl up into her arms and cradled her to her chest.

"It's okay," she whispered into her soft head, "Mama's here."

Sara began to sway, rocking her back and forth, and she felt the baby shudder a breath against her.

It was only then she realized that Owen was standing behind her.

"Her name is Juniper," Sara said tentatively. "I don't know how I know that, but…" She trailed off.

"You're right," Owen said. "It was the only name we could agree on."

His fingers brushed the top of Sara's spine in a supportive gesture. She could sense him behind her, ready to catch her if she fell. If she had been involved in something criminal, how could she have risked hurting her child? Then it hit her—all this time, Owen had known she had a daughter and hadn't told her. She stepped forward, away from his touch.

"She's healthy and strong," Owen said. "She only started pulling herself up to standing a few days ago, which is early. But she doesn't crawl yet. She sort of half swims across the floor. The pediatrician said some babies skip crawling and go straight to walking."

Juniper's breathing had settled, but when Sara looked down, her eyes were still wide open, taking in the world.

"She only started sleeping through the night back in November," he went on. "Usually I get a good six or even seven hours now, but sometimes she wakes up in the night like tonight. Her appetite is great, but I haven't had much success getting her to eat solid foods yet."

Owen kept talking, quickly, almost as if he was afraid of what would happen if he stopped. But there was something else in his tone too. It was clear he loved Juniper with all his heart and wanted to reassure Sara that her little girl had been well cared for.

"I've tried carrot and squash," Owen continued. "Travis suggested I try this rice formula his son, Dominic, liked."

"How old is she?" Sara asked.

"Seven and a half months," he said.

Sara turned to face him and for the first time really saw the room they were in. She guessed it was Jess and Travis's bedroom. Laundry was piled on the large bed, and toys covered the floor. She looked up at Owen. "So when I disappeared, she was…" Her words trailed off as fresh tears choked her voice.

"Only six weeks old," he said.

She closed her eyes tightly for a moment, the weight of knowing she'd missed so much of her child's life pressing against her heart and making it hard to breathe.

"I'm sorry," Owen said, and she didn't know what he was apologizing for. For not telling her sooner? For the fact they'd let their relationship fall apart when there was a baby involved?

She tried to pray but couldn't find the words to begin to turn her fears into faith. For months she'd been praying for answers, but did she really want them now? During all the time that Sara had wondered who she was, she'd never imagined she might be someone she didn't like. Someone who'd let her relationship fall apart. Someone who might've committed a crime. Someone who'd potentially let her own selfishness hurt her child.

What if her memories all came back and she hated the truth about who she was?

There was a gentle knock on the door frame behind her. She opened her eyes and turned. It was Jess.

"Sara, I set up the bed for you in the attic," Jess said, "in case you want to rest a bit before Anne gets here. Travis reminded me that we have this little bedside crib he used to use when our daughter Willow was too frightened to sleep alone. He stepped in as a father for Willow and Dominic a few years ago after their parents died, then later we adopted them. One wall of the crib slides up and down so that Juniper can be in her crib but still be close by."

"Thank you," Sara said.

Her mind was numb and overwhelmed from the sheer number of questions that flooded it. The only thing she knew for sure was she needed to do everything in her power to protect and care for the once-forgotten baby in her arms. Awkwardly, Owen excused himself and went downstairs, saying he was going to get Juniper a bottle. Sara followed Jess down the hallway, up a second flight of stairs and into a wide A-frame attic bedroom with slanted ceilings. Two thirds of the space was filled with old camping equipment, boxes of clothes, bikes, trikes and summer toys. But at one end, a large screen divided off a private area, where she found a double bed with a colorful quilt on it underneath a small round window that looked out into the night. The crib Jess had told her about was nestled to one side. Owen returned with the bottle, then he left along with Jess to wait for the doctor. She imagined he and his friends had a lot to talk about too.

She knew so little about this family—the former cop, Travis, and the current cop, Jess, with their two adopted children and new little baby—but they'd welcomed her into their home just as the Zooks had. Owen trusted Travis and Jess.

And for some reason, something deep inside her that seemed to defy all logic still trusted Owen.

Juniper finished her bottle and fell back asleep. But Sara continued to hold her until she felt the baby grow heavy in her arms and started to nod off herself. She set Juniper down in the bedside crib and then stretched out on the bed beside her, still fully clothed in the outfit she'd borrowed from Jess, and looked at her baby girl. Sara's eyelids battled sleep; she was half-afraid that if she let her eyes close, she'd wake up back on the farm having forgotten her daughter again.

She didn't know when she'd fallen asleep, but suddenly she was dreaming. As usual, she was in a hospital bed and could hear a baby crying. But this time when she looked over, Sara could see Juniper beside her. The tiny baby was only hours old. Her skin was red and new.

Her little arms waved and her legs kicked, as if trying to shake off her tiny white booties and gloves.

Like she was excited to be alive.

A fierce and protective love surged through Sara's heart. She knew she'd do anything in her power to keep her safe.

Then, in what was either her memory or dream—or both—she looked to her left and saw Owen, disheveled and exhausted, sleeping upright in an uncomfortable-looking chair in the corner of the room, like a sentry guarding the door.

Then she woke up to find pale predawn light filtering through the window above her head, a soft quilt laying over her and Owen dozing uncomfortably in a folding camp chair that he'd stationed between the corner of the divider screen and the stairs. His green eyes opened, his gaze met hers and for a long moment he just stared at her in a mixture of confusion and wonderment, as if he was afraid to speak, in case he discovered she wasn't really there and he was dreaming. An unknown feeling ached in her chest. And for the first time, she had a glimpse at how much he'd missed her.

Then he blinked.

"Sara!" he said and stood quickly. "Hi! You're awake!"

"Good morning," she said. She pushed the quilt off her and swung her legs over the edge of the bed. "Did you put the blanket over me?"

He blushed slightly. "I did. Quilting used to be a hobby of yours. You made some really beautiful ones back in the day."

"Huh." She'd loved sewing quilts with Hadassah too.

Maybe she wasn't completely different from the person she used to be.

Instinctively, she reached for the gold ring on the chain around her neck, like she did every morning. Owen noticed.

"Sorry," he said. "I don't know if it was uncomfortable to sleep with that on, but I didn't want to take it off without asking."

"I never take it off," she said and rolled the smooth gold ring around in her fingers. It was cool to the touch. Then she let it fall back onto her chest. "I thought a doctor was coming?"

"She did," Owen said. "She's here now and asleep on the couch in Jess's office. You were asleep, and Anne said it was best to let you rest. Her son works in movie makeup and costuming, so she also brought a couple of trunks of clothes and wigs and things, to help change up your look."

She wasn't sure she wanted to change up her look. There was a simple and functional beauty to the *plain* way the Amish dressed. Also, changing her appearance implied she'd be hiding here for a while. And while she'd gratefully accepted the Tatlows' hospitality, now that she'd actually managed to get some sleep, she wasn't sure how long she wanted to just hide out and let strangers try to unravel the mystery of her life.

Owen's phone began to ring. He pulled it from his pocket quickly, frowned and pushed a button to shut it off. But not before Juniper stirred. He slid it back in his pocket.

"Everything okay?" Sara asked.

"Yeah," he said. "Like I told you yesterday, I'm the

interim mayor. It's a part-time job, which is why I also run a hardware store." He rubbed his hand over the back of his neck. "Okay, I feel ridiculous even mentioning it, but I woke up to a bunch of people texting me with their ideas for big, special things we can add to the winter fair. Nothing that can't wait until tomorrow. The one thing you can say about Kilpatrick is people dream big."

Juniper began to cry. The sound was faint at first, hesitant and halting, as if she was trying to decide whether to gear up for a full-on wail. Sara pushed herself to her feet, but Owen got there first and scooped their daughter up into his arms.

"I'll change her real quick, if you want to get yourself turned around to see Anne," he said. He took Juniper to a changing table that had been set up on the other side of the divider. "How are you feeling?"

"Achy," she admitted. Her whole body hurt. "And confused."

Owen turned away from her and busied himself with getting their baby changed into fresh clothes. Thoughts and feelings from the day before began to filter through her mind like puzzle pieces made of confetti and trapped inside a snow globe. Nothing made sense. She was a military intelligence officer and had been estranged from Owen and had a child. But she'd also been running from someone who shot her in the head. Then a different woman had been found dead in her car, with her wallet and phone. That woman had been identified as her, somehow, and buried in her grave. Then two men with guns had shown up at the farmhouse looking for something.

"I'm missing something," she said, half to herself. "Last night, you all sat around talking about me like I was just some case file you were looking at. But I know, in my gut, that none of you had the whole picture. There's something you were all missing."

Even from the side view, she could see a deep frown crease Owen's face. He did that, she realized, when he didn't agree with her. She'd noticed it the night before. He didn't say anything, just scrunched up his face in silent protest.

It was irritating.

"You think I'm wrong," she said.

"I didn't say anything," Owen said.

"You didn't need to. It was written all over your face."

His eyes widened, and somehow she suspected they'd had this exact argument countless times before. That he didn't actually speak when he disagreed with her, so that he couldn't be accused of taking a side, but still made his feelings clearly known.

"For all we know, I was never the target these criminals were after," she added. "This could all be some very tragic misunderstanding."

"A tragic misunderstanding," he repeated. He picked Juniper up off the changing table and turned to face her, with Juniper propped up in his arms so Sara could see her face.

"Weren't you the guy who just yesterday was telling me to trust my gut?" she asked. "My gut doesn't think the military intelligence angle thing I overheard you talking about feels right. Maybe this other woman was the target all along, and I was shot by mistake."

"That doesn't make sense," Owen said.

"Nothing makes sense right now though," she shot back.

"Right, but your theory is ridiculous."

"Ridiculous?" Her voice rose.

"I've already put a call in to the dentist who identified the body as yours," he went on, like she hadn't spoken. "I'll pop over to his place while you're resting. Dr. Freck has been around since I was a kid and must be well into his seventies. Hopefully he'll let me look at the dental records he used to identify the body as yours. Meanwhile, Jess and Travis are going to talk to some of their contacts and do their own investigating."

She didn't know what she'd thought she'd been looking for when she'd walked for miles to find this man. But it wasn't this.

"They've got kids to worry about," she said. "It would make more sense for me to just go to the police station and let whichever cop has been assigned to my apparent murder sort this out," Sara said. "Because what I don't want is any more of this cloak-and-dagger stuff, where I keep feeling like you know things you're not telling me. I don't know if we used to keep secrets from each other. I'm guessing we did. But I've been honest with you and told you everything I know. And I expect you to do the same to me."

"I thought you trusted me," he said.

"I do," she said. Her arms crossed. "But that doesn't mean you won't lose that trust in a heartbeat if you keep treating me like you think I'm helpless and incompetent."

"In all the time I've known you, I've never once

thought of you as either helpless or incompetent," Owen said, growing louder.

"Then why can't I go to the police?"

"Jess and Travis are the—"

"Owen!" she cut him off. "Stop waffling and be straight with me."

"Fine," he said. "Anne says I'm not supposed to upset you, but apparently not telling you things gets you worked up too. Maybe you're wanted by the police or wrapped up in some criminal operation. Because last night, Jess discovered that Beau and Coop are police officers from Sudbury."

She felt her eyes widen.

"That's right, those men who broke into the farm-house, tried to kidnap you and shot at me are cops."

Owen watched as the color drained from Sara's face.

Anne had specifically warned him to be gentle with Sara and keep her calm until Anne had the opportunity to assess her concussion, just in case her ordeal yesterday had worsened it. And here he'd already messed that up. But in all the time he'd spent missing Sara, he'd forgotten just how much she'd gotten under his skin.

"Wow," Sara said, after taking a beat. "So maybe I'm a criminal."

"You're not," he said automatically.

Her blue eyes widened. She looked up at him under thick dark lashes.

"Do you know that for a fact?" she asked. "Or is that your gut talking?"

"Just my gut," he admitted.

"And do I usually trust your gut?"

He chuckled, despite himself. "No, actually. You think I'm wishy-washy."

She laughed then grabbed at her lips as if to catch it. "I'm sorry."

"No, it's okay," he said. "It's good to hear you laugh."

Juniper started to fuss, reminding them both that she hadn't been fed yet. The fleeting but beautiful smile slipped from Sara's lips as she looked at her daughter, and it was like he could see her mentally calculating what would happen to their relationship if they went to the police.

Would she be detained? Arrested? Ripped away from her daughter as this whole thing was sorted out?

"Here, why don't you take her," Owen said, "and I'll go get her a bottle."

Sara reached for her, and as he passed Juniper into her arms, he felt Sara's fingers brush against his. Suddenly, something inside him wanted to open his arms and envelop Sara and Juniper into them and promise them both it was all going to be okay.

But instead, he turned away and went downstairs to get the bottle.

The second floor of the house was still dark and quiet. But on the main floor, a light was on in the kitchen, where Travis was holding baby Lottie and Anne was making tea. In a rumpled plaid shirt and jeans, Travis looked like he'd gotten even less sleep than Owen had. Anne offered Owen the remaining water in the kettle to make a bottle, then said she'd take it up to Sara. Jess appeared and took Lottie from Travis and went to feed her.

Travis glanced at Owen. "I'm about to step outside for a bit," he said. "Want to join me?"

Owen nodded. "Sure."

He grabbed his coat off a hook by the door and followed Travis outside. The Tatlows' farmhouse had a long and sweeping front porch with a railing and a porch swing. Travis leaned against the railing and looked out at the trees. Owen joined him. And together they stood side by side in silence for a long minute, looking out at the golden sunlight creeping in through snow-capped trees. Travis had draped his right hand over the edge with two fingers outstretched. He must've noticed Owen track the gesture because Travis looked down at his own hand self-consciously and chuckled.

"I used to smoke," Travis said. "A very long time ago, before my life got straightened out. When I became a detective working with the special victims cases, I switched from smoking to high-caffeine energy drinks instead because it was much more socially acceptable. It wasn't until I got on the wrong side of a pretty nasty individual and ended up here in witness protection that I managed to kick the caffeine too and came to some peace within myself."

"I had no idea you were in witness protection," Owen said.

"That's how I reconnected with Jess," Travis said. "A few years ago someone stole a whole bunch of RCMP witness-protection files and auctioned them off online. One of them was mine. Jess and a group of law enforcement officers formed a small task force, off the grid, to protect those involved and came here to convince me to run and hide. But by that point I was raising Willow and Dominic and couldn't imagine leaving them."

"Wow," Owen said. "What did you do?"

"We worked together and caught the guy who was after me," he said. "Like I've told you, my wife is amazing. She's tough and tenacious. If anyone can figure out what's going on with Officer Beau and Officer Coop, it's her. Jess has already been on the horn with their police chief, who's assured her they've been dragged in for questioning. She didn't mention anything about what Sara experienced, but she didn't need to. Them showing up here, illegally showing off their guns like that, trying to muscle their way into our home is more than enough. Even if the chief doesn't get anything out of them, it'll still tie them up for hours and keep them away from Kilpatrick. So for now, that's one less thing we have to worry about."

Travis sighed.

"What I don't get is how cops from Sudbury could possibly have any jurisdiction over a woman living over five hours away," he added. "I don't know if they're corrupt cops who are going about catching a criminal the wrong way. Or if they're after Sara for some more nefarious reason. But either way, they're going to regret trying to bluff their way into our house."

Travis smiled a thin-lipped grin. Then he asked, "How's Sara?"

"I don't know," Owen admitted. "She seems fine— shaken but fine. I imagine she's incredibly sore from her trek yesterday. Not to mention terrified. But she's never been one to whine. She always took whatever came at her and rolled with it."

Travis nodded. It was a simple enough gesture. But something about it put Owen on edge and reminded him that Travis's former detective days weren't anywhere near as far behind him as he liked to think.

"Clearly she was dealing with something major before her disappearance that she didn't tell you about," Travis said.

Unless Sara was right, and she was attacked by mistake.

"Do you think it's possible it was something criminal?" Travis added.

"No, I don't think so," Owen said. When Travis didn't say anything, Owen added, "Sara asked me the same thing."

"Is it possible she faked her own death?" Travis asked. "Or was somehow involved in the death of the woman now in her grave? Maybe she tried to disappear and wanted you to think she was dead. Maybe she was doing something illegal and was double-crossed by whoever shot her."

Owen felt his jaw clench but couldn't find the right words.

"Are you sure she has amnesia?" Trevor asked. "Could she be faking it?"

He'd floated the words across the porch as gently as if they were a beach ball. Yet Owen wanted to pop it and send it falling to the ground.

"Yes, I believe she has amnesia," Owen said emphatically. "No, I don't believe for one second she's faking it. And for that matter, I don't believe she killed anyone, hurt anyone, tried to fake her death or was involved in anything illegal."

"It's the most logical explanation," Travis said, "especially considering she was working in military intelligence."

"I don't care," Owen said. "She has a good heart. Her faith in God was real. She cared about serving her county and helping people. If anything, it's more likely she was attacked for trying to help someone. Whatever is going on, she's the victim."

"And you're sure about that?" Travis asked.

"One thousand percent," Owen said.

The sun rose higher above the trees. The men walked back into the house. Sara and Anne were waiting for them in the living room, and both stood when they walked in. Sara had gotten changed into a long yellow dress with a white fabric wrap that reminded him of daisies, along with a pair of dark green leggings and a scarf tied over her head. The outfit was totally modern and yet reminded him of the Amish clothes she'd been wearing the day before so much it was like she was trying to remake it. Sara's black shoulder-length hair was much longer and thicker now, with loose curls that fell down to her waist. He must've stared because she self-consciously reached for a strand and twirled it between her fingers. His mouth went dry.

"They're hair extensions," Sara said. "Does it look okay?"

"You look wonderful," he said honestly.

Then he looked at his daughter. Juniper was wearing a matching yellow dress and leggings and was tucked onto Sara's hip. Sara stretched her out for Owen to take her. He took Juniper into his hands, and as he did so their fingertips touched, sending electricity tingling through his skin. He stepped back.

"Good news is Sara's got a clean bill of health," Anne said. "She's incredibly strong. Not many people could do what she did yesterday. My biggest focus right now is encouraging her to remember to eat, sleep and pace herself."

"As for my memory loss, Anne said the same thing Dr. Amos said," Sara added. "It may come back in pieces or all at once. But I might never remember some things or whole parts of my past at all."

There was a simplicity and vulnerability to her words that made something prick painfully in his chest.

Lord, please heal her mind and make her whole.

They all walked into the kitchen. The room was square and warm with teal cabinets and burnt-orange walls covered in colorful children's art. Travis sat at the large round table under the tall windows with a girl who seemed to be about six with waves of unruly, taffy-colored hair and a smiling boy in a high chair who looked about two and a half. Jess stood by the counter bouncing baby Lottie. Containers of juices, milks and cereal covered the table. Hard-boiled eggs rolled cheerfully in boiling water on the stove.

"Sara, this is Willow," Owen said, gesturing first to the small girl with the curious face and billowing hair and then to the little boy in the high chair, "and this is Dominic. Guys, this is Juniper's mommy, Sara."

Willow looked down at her toast and scowled. "That's not Juniper's mommy." Her words were matter-of-fact, but Owen noticed her lips trembled slightly. "Juniper's mommy is dead, and people who are dead stay dead."

Every adult in the room seemed to freeze at once. Travis and Jess shared a worried glance as Sara pulled an empty chair over beside Willow's and sat down in it sideways.

"You're absolutely right," she said seriously, looking at the little girl. "People who are dead stay dead."

Willow's eyes flickered to her face. Confusion filled their depths.

"But you know how people, even adults, make mistakes sometimes?" Sara asked.

Willow paused as if wondering what she'd be committing herself to in answering the question. Finally, she nodded. "Yeah?"

"Well, I got lost," Sara said, "very, very lost. In fact, I was so lost, for so long, that everybody made a mistake and thought I was dead. Which is not a normal thing that happens to people, but it happened to me."

Willow's lips twitched for a moment. Then she nodded as if she'd decided something important.

"I'm sorry you were lost," Willow said. "Was it scary?"

"It was very scary," Sara said, "but thankfully now I've been found."

And Owen felt the painful prick in his chest that he had felt earlier grow deeper.

After breakfast, Travis packed the two older kids up to take them to day care and school before heading to open the bookstore he ran on Main Street. The theory was that on the slim possibility they were still being watched by someone, it would be best to pretend everything was business as usual. Anne too left to head home, promising she'd check in with them later.

Owen had planned to go to the dentist's office alone after breakfast to inquire about the medical records. Dr. Freck's dental office was based on the main floor of his huge house, just off Main Street. Owen's calls to both had gone unanswered, but whether Dr. Freck was at home or in his office, Owen hoped to catch him before he started the day.

But to his frustration, Sara wanted to go too.

"These are my dental records we're talking about," she insisted as they cleaned up the kitchen. "I'll recognize them and know immediately if something is up."

"But what if whoever's behind this sees you with me?"

"We have no reason to believe that Coop and Beau aren't working alone," she countered, "or that if they are working for someone, whoever they're working with is here in Kilpatrick. Sudbury is several hours away from here, as is Ottawa."

He opened his mouth to argue, but her hands snapped to her hips.

"The sooner we get this mystery solved, the sooner this will all be over," Sara added. "I don't know about you, but I want this whole thing wrapped up as quickly as possible. There's been a mystery woman buried in my grave for six months, and I don't want to delay finding out who she is or giving her family closure a moment longer than necessary."

He couldn't disagree with that. But then what? Would Sara be in jail? Would she try to return to her life back in Ottawa? Or go back to live with the Amish? What would happen to her, to him and to Juniper?

In the end, it was decided that Owen would go ahead in his truck alone, with Jess and Sara following from behind in the Taltows' SUV. The women would drop both Lottie and Juniper off to Travis at the bookstore and then meet Owen at the dentist's office. He'd go in by himself to see Dr. Freck, but Sara would be nearby to join him if and when they decided. Meanwhile, Jess would casually tell anyone who asked that Sara was in town to help out with the kids. It was as good a plan as any and better than most.

He transferred Juniper's car seat from the back seat of his double-cab truck to Jess's SUV and then drove down the Tatlows' long and private unpaved road onto the small rural highway that would lead him back into town. It was only then that he remembered the snowmobile he'd restored that was now lost somewhere at the bottom of the pond on their property. Sara had been so annoyed by the fact he'd never made time to finish restoring it and had instead left it in pieces littering their tiny garage. And then, once she'd gone, he'd thrown himself into it. Not to spite her in any way, but because he'd needed something to do with his hands. Something to stop himself from thinking about her.

The sky was an unsettling shade of gray that made him think of a dirty car windshield in winter. Thick snow swirled down around him as he drove. The road was pretty much empty and no different than usual, except for the small shape of Jess's SUV on the road behind him.

No matter how many times he drove through Kilpatrick, he never failed to be struck by just how beautiful it was. Every individual business and store on Main Street was unique, with its own different windows and window boxes, wooden or brick facades, and awnings covered with snow.

When he'd checked his phone that morning, it had

been filled with messages and texts from various business owners in town, eager to talk to him about all their wonderfully lavish ideas for the upcoming winter fair they'd come up with at the party the night before. Odd to think that the last time he'd driven down this road, the town's financial difficulties and the budget of the winter fair had weighed heavily on his mind. Now those things barely made a dent.

He pulled off halfway down the street onto a boulevard that was part business and part residential. Dr. Grover Freck's office was on the ground floor of a large yellow mansion that had seen better days, with dark brown wooden trim and a wooded hill to the back. There were no lights on upstairs, but a dim light was visible in the dentist's office around back.

He parked on the street in front of the building. When he went to knock on the front door, it swung open under his touch. He stepped inside.

"Hello!" he called. "Dr. Freck? It's Owen Kilpatrick. You in?"

No answer. He stepped into the waiting room and walked past the same cracked plastic couches, faded posters and scribbled-on books that he remembered from childhood.

"Hello?" he called again.

The door to the examination room was ajar. He pushed it open, and the tinny smell of medical supplies filled his senses. The side door to Dr. Freck's office lay half-open.

"Hello?" he called again. "Dr. Freck?"

An odd bright red pinpoint of light flashed against the window glass. Instinctively, he glanced toward the window and saw a large black silhouette of a man standing on the hill.

The red dot of a sniper's rifle scope darted like a minnow across the wall toward him.

Owen hit the floor as the window exploded in a spray of glass.

FIVE

Glass cascaded across the floor, raining down over Owen as the window caved in. The sniper fired again, and a second bullet struck the wall, shattering the plaster.

Owen's heart lurched, and adrenaline pounded through his veins. Had Jess and Juniper pulled up yet? He had to battle the urge to jump up and run outside to make sure they were all right. Instead he focused on the fact a light was on in the dentist's office. Sara was with Jess. But his childhood dentist had to be in his seventies. If he was in there, he'd need help getting out alive.

"Dr. Freck!" Owen called. "Shout if you can hear me!"

Owen prayed for God's help and protection. He pushed across the floor, keeping as low to the ground as possible, in an odd swimming motion reminiscent of Juniper's recent attempts to crawl.

A third shot flew. This one ricocheted off the counter, sending a tray of metal dental tools flying onto the floor in front of him. The sniper was so far away he couldn't hear the shots themselves ring out, only see the impact of them exploding the world around him. Whoever was firing was being deliberate and calculating—and using a silencer.

He heard what sounded like two shots take out the window in the adjacent room and imbed themselves in the wall. Then silence fell. He pushed the office door open and crawled through. Cold wind whipped through the shattered remains where the window had once been. Glass littered the floor here as well. But the faint smell of what seemed to be burning plastic filled the air. He looked to his right. There in the white ashes of a wood-burning stove were what looked like the twisted remains of dental X-rays.

Owen climbed to his feet. Then he saw Dr. Freck. The old man was sitting slumped at his desk with his head on his chest like he'd just sat down and nodded off to sleep.

"Dr. Freck!" Owen's voice rose. "Wake up!"

Staying low, he hurried across the office and tapped the man on the shoulder, barely resisting the urge to shake him. "We've got to go!"

The elderly man didn't move. Only then did Owen see the bullet wound. The man had been shot in the temple at a distance, probably from one of the same bullets that had taken out the window. But the wound was bloodless. Owen touched the man's arm. It was stiff, and his skin was cold to the touch. Rigor mortis had already set in.

Dr. Freck was not only already dead, but by the look of things, he had been dead for hours. Owen had seen the man alive and well, albeit through a window, at a party with the town muckety-mucks not more than nine or ten hours ago. It appeared he'd come home, gone to his office, sat down at his desk and peacefully died in his sleep.

Which made no sense. Especially considering the sniper who'd fired three bullets into the building so far and the mysterious fire in the grate.

Help me, Lord. I am so confused and lost right now. Help me get justice and make it out of here alive.

The gunman on the hill behind the dentist's office had yet to fire again. Owen glanced to the window and scanned for the figure he'd seen before. Was he reloading? Had he finished what he'd set out to do?

Either way, Owen wasn't going to wait to find out.

Staying low, he ran through the emergency fire exit out into a side alley, sending the fire alarm screaming. He ran toward the street. Jess's SUV was parked behind his truck. The cop had already jumped out and had her cell phone to her ear.

"What's happening?" Jess shouted over the blaring siren. "We heard breaking glass then a fire alarm."

"Someone fired multiple shots into the building," Owen said. "Dr. Freck is dead. But he's been dead for hours."

She blinked. "Where's Dr. Freck now?"

"In his office," he said. "Looks like a heart attack."

How did that make any sense? Then it struck him—could the sniper be using the gunfire to disguise how long Dr. Freck had been dead?

"Do we still have an active shooter situation?" Jess asked.

"I don't think so," he said. "He stopped firing."

"Anyone else in the building? Anyone with injuries?"

"No and no. Building seems empty."

"Got it," Jess said. "Stay here. I have to call this in and secure the scene. Travis is at the bookstore. Head there, and you'll be safe."

Jess turned and ran to secure the building, shouting into her phone as she went.

"Owen," Sara said. "Are you okay? Are you hurt?"

Sara's voice pulled his attention to the vehicle. He leaned down and looked in. Sara was in the passenger seat. She looked so concerned about him that he felt his breath catch in his throat.

"I'm fine," he said and turned away. "Don't worry about me."

He used to hate it when she worried about him. It was his job to be the strong one, and whenever she'd worried about him, it had made him feel like he was failing her somehow.

A glimmer of light flashed on the hill from where the shots had come. Had the sniper returned? He shifted to see a figure disappearing between the trees.

The criminal was still there and was now on the run.

Owen glanced at Sara. Jess had left the keys dangling in the ignition.

"Do you remember how to drive?" he asked.

"Yeah," Sara said. There wasn't a flicker of doubt in her eyes.

He reached into his jeans' pocket and pulled out a small pocketknife. "Here, take this—"

"I'm not going to wield a weapon on another human being—"

"Just take it," he cut her off. "Please. I need you to be safe."

She might've embraced a more pacifist way of life, but they didn't have time for that now. He breathed a sigh of relief as she took it from his hand and slid it into her pocket.

"Stay safe," he added. "I spotted a guy on the hill. Whether he's the gunman or a witness, I can't let him get away."

"Owen, no..." Sara started.

He turned and ran toward the hill.

"Owen!" she yelled. "Stop!"

He didn't pause or even let himself look back. He couldn't let this man get away. He had to stop whoever was behind this and had shot up Dr. Freck's office, killed the unknown woman in Sara's grave, and shot Sara herself.

This might be his only opportunity to find out who'd robbed Sara of her memories and Juniper of her mother, and why.

It might be now or never—and Owen couldn't let him get away.

He ran past the dentist's office, up the hill and toward the empty space in the tree line where he'd seen the figure disappear. His legs pushed through the knee-deep snow, and he prayed with every step. Fierce wind beat against his body. He reached the top of the hill, panting. Thick trees spread out ahead of him. Whoever he'd spotted was nowhere to be seen, leaving nothing but broken branches and scuffed ground to show where the person had been. Owen trudged on, following the trail as best he could even as the snow swirled around him, wiping the footprints away.

A crack sounded in the trees to his right. He turned to see a fist. The blow came out of nowhere. The hard and fast sucker punch knocked him to the ground. Stars filled his eyes. His lungs struggled to catch breaths. Why would the man punch him when he could've just shot him or run?

A large shape in a ski mask loomed above him.

"I'm only taking pity on you, because you don't know who she really is," a distorted voice boomed at the edges of his pain-filled skull. "Our issue is with her. Not with you. This is your only warning, Stop helping her, and we'll leave you alone. Otherwise both you and your baby will die."

No!

The single word filled Owen's heart.

Whatever Sara had done, he was going to help her find out the truth, even if it ended with her behind bars.

Even if it meant Juniper would lose her mother.

The man turned and ran. Owen pushed himself to his feet, but before he could follow him, he heard the sound of a snowmobile roar.

His attacker had gotten away.

Frustration burned at the back of Owen's throat. He turned toward the office once again. Swirling snow stung his eyes, even as dark spots still blinded his gaze. He reached the edge of the tree line and looked down.

Two police cars and an ambulance had converged on the dentist's office below.

But there was no sign of Sara and the SUV. Desperately, he scanned the street from one end to the other.

Sara was gone.

* * *

The barrel of a gun pressed sharply into Sara's side. Tears filled her eyes, blurring her vision of the snow-covered trees outside the windshield of the SUV.

"Just keep driving," the woman in the long dark coat ordered. "Now you're going to do exactly what I say. Otherwise, I can't promise you'll make it out of here alive."

Help me, Lord, and hear my prayer, Sara implored desperately. *You are my refuge and my protector in times of danger.*

The kidnapping had happened so quickly that Sara's panicked, terrified brain was still too numb from shock to put the pieces together about what was going on. She gasped a deep breath and ordered herself to focus.

She knew that Owen had run up the hill and disappeared into the trees. She'd then been shifting her body from the passenger's seat into the driver's seat of Jess's SUV when she heard the sound of the passenger door opening behind her and a pleasant female voice asked if she was okay.

Then the passenger door had slammed shut before Sara could even respond, and she'd turned back to see the barrel of a gun pointed at her below the eye level of anyone glancing in. The stranger had told her to drive or she'd open fire. Sara started driving.

The whole thing had taken mere seconds.

The kidnapper was directing her to drive out of town and into the empty countryside. But she didn't seem to be directing Sara anywhere in particular. Rather, she seemed focused on taking her away from town and somewhere isolated.

"I don't know who you are or what you want," Sara said, surprised to hear the strength and courage filling her own voice. "But put the gun down and we can find way to work this out without the need for violence."

The woman beside her didn't speak for a long moment. Silence filled the vehicle, punctuated only by the sound of the engine rattling, the tires rolling over the ice and the wind howling outside. For the first time, Sara risked a good solid look at the woman who'd taken her hostage.

She had angular features with long, straight dark hair and wore impeccable makeup. But there was something pinched and tight about the woman's face, like she was used to scowling, and Sara could tell her shoulders were sharp under her expensive wool coat. She didn't look strong or confident. She looked angry and desperate.

"Don't play games with me," the woman said. "You know exactly what this is about. You took something that didn't belong to you, and I'm just here to get it back."

What?

"You think I stole something?" Sara asked. Was this woman telling the truth? Had Sara really been a thief? "What did I steal?"

The woman swore angrily. "Don't play dumb!" she snapped. "You know exactly what this is about, Sara. Just give me those files, and this will all be over."

"What files?" Sara asked as curiosity temporarily overtook fear. "You mean like paper files? I don't have any paper files!"

Any paper she'd had on her when she'd been shot was long gone before she was found.

"I mean like on a memory stick!" The woman grew louder.

Well, Sara was pretty sure she hadn't had a memory stick on her when she was found either. Had she been carrying the files some other way? If so, where were they now?

Again, she prayed for wisdom.

"I have amnesia," Sara said, going straight for the truth. "I have a major brain injury. I don't know who you are or what these files are you're talking about."

The woman sat back in her seat. Apparently this news was so unexpected it had knocked the wind out of her. The gun shifted from Sara's side, and the woman pulled it back, just outside Sara's reach.

The woman reached into her pocket, pulled out her phone and typed something with one hand. Sara eased her foot off the accelerator just a little, trying to slow the vehicle's speed without the woman noticing.

Then Sara eased her left hand off the steering wheel and slid her fingers into her pocket for the small knife Owen has pressed into her hand. She felt for the small, smooth shape and nudged it into the cuff of her jacket sleeve. Then she slowly brought her hand around.

"Well, that would explain why you just popped off the map and never called me!" her kidnapper said. "We're actually old friends. I can't believe you don't remember me."

The woman's tone of voice had switched suddenly. It was now sweet—too sweet—and apologetic, but still sent an uncomfortable shiver up her spine.

"I'm Casey," the woman said unconvincingly, with a big smile that didn't even begin to touch the anger in her eyes. "Casey Brown. We met at the city pool and used to swim laps at five in the morning together? I'm a lawyer? Sara, we were sharing an apartment when Owen came along, and you ditched our friendship to be with him."

Sudden memories flooded Sara's mind, overwhelming her senses. She jolted so suddenly she felt the precariously hidden knife slip from her sleeve and clatter down the side of her seat, just inches away from her leg. She remembered the smell of the pool's chlorine in the early morning and the refreshing chill of the water on her skin as she dived in and pushed her limbs through the water. She remembered the dread in her stomach as she walked up her apartment steps, boxes in hands, knowing her roommate was upset with her.

But the face of the woman beside her was still a mystery.

"I don't remember you," Sara said, "and if we were really friends, put the gun down."

"I'm really sorry, Sara," Casey said, "but you've clearly forgotten you don't trust Owen. In fact, you showed up at my office in August and asked me to draw up papers suing for full custody of Juniper and a restraining order to keep him from ever coming near you or Juniper again."

No, no—that couldn't be true.

"You even had me draw up legal papers demanding the full disclosure of all his assets because you thought he was lying to you about property and money," she went on. "When I thought you'd died, I took them to the police and told them I was sure he'd killed you."

Owen's gentle green eyes and kind smile filled her

mind. No, it wasn't true. She'd have never done that to Owen. She'd have never tried to file such obviously false allegations against him. She'd have never tried to keep him from seeing his daughter. Would she?

"Then after you disappeared, some really scary men ambushed me outside my apartment," her kidnapper went on. "They told me you'd hacked a government database and stolen some high-security military files to sell to them. But you double-crossed them and kept the money. They figured as your lawyer, I might have them. They threatened to kill me and my parents if I didn't find them."

No, no, she had to be lying. She didn't believe it. She couldn't believe it.

"I don't know what you're talking about," Sara said.

"I want my life back!" her kidnapper yelled. She waved the weapon around, inches from Sara's face. A desperate sincerity rang through her voice. "I'm sick of being threatened! I'm sick of living in fear! You get me those files, I turn them over and my life goes back to normal. That's all I care about. So if I have to kill Owen, your baby and everyone you care about to do that, then I will!"

And Sara suddenly knew two things in her gut. The first was that, maybe for the first time during this whole encounter, her kidnapper was telling the absolute truth. The second was that she was far less skilled with a gun than she had once been.

"But I'm not going to let you hurt them," she said.

She heard a click and felt the gun press against her temple.

"This is not a negotiation." Casey's voice went cold.

"You're going to get me those files, or you won't like the consequences."

Certainty swept over Sara, flooding her heart with peace and her instincts with military precision. She felt like someone who'd been tossed into a river suddenly remembering she knew how to swim.

With one hand, Sara yanked the steering wheel hard to the left, placing her foot on the brake, tapping it to help control the spin. With the other hand, she grabbed the woman's wrist and smacked it hard against the dashboard. Casey yelped in pain, and the gun fell from her grasp.

Sara grabbed it, aimed past Casey and fired at the door. Her precision bullet flew through the locking mechanism and the door fell open. Only then did Sara fully hit the brakes. The car lurched to a stop, Sara leveled a quick blow to the woman's jaw, which would stun her, Sara knew, but not seriously hurt her. While Casey was still reeling, Sara grabbed for the knife and, in a single quick and clean motion, sliced Casey's seat belt free instead of reaching over to unbuckle it. Sara spun around on her seat, raised her legs and kicked hard, sending her kidnapper flying backward out of the passenger door and tumbling out onto the road.

Sara spun back, hit the gas and sped down the road toward Kilpatrick.

A quick, simple and efficient drop-off, perfectly executed, with limited damage to the target.

The words hovered in the back of her mind like a foreign language. How had that even been possible? How had she known how to do that? She glanced back to see Casey stumble to her feet and start shouting into her cell phone.

Within minutes, she saw Owen's truck racing down the highway toward her. She hit the brakes, and so did he. The vehicles swerved to a stop within feet of each other. Owen leaped out of the driver's seat and started toward her, with Travis close on his heels. She opened the door and stumbled out onto the road, and discovered her limbs were so shaken she could barely stand.

Only then did the full impact of what had just happened strike her mind.

A woman who claimed to be from her past had called her a thief and accused her of trying to destroy Owen financially and take his daughter from him. And Sara had somehow known how to not only disarm her, shoot a car door open and quite literally kick her out of the vehicle without causing her serious injury.

Both men were shouting to her at once, their voices overlapping as one.

"Sara!"

"Are you okay?"

"What happened?"

"Is everyone okay?"

"I'm fine!" she shouted. "The kidnapper got away. Where are Juniper and Lottie?"

"Safe," Travis said, "with a trusted friend."

"How did you find me?"

"There's a GPS tracker installed in the SUV," Travis said.

Sara felt Owen brush her shoulder, and she threw her arms around him.

"Hey, it's okay," Owen said. He held her tightly and she shuddered a breath. "You're okay. I've got you."

But no, it wasn't okay.

She pulled back out of Owen's embrace just enough to look into his face. But somehow she couldn't bring herself to look him in the eyes.

"Who am I?" she asked.

"You're Sara Kilpatrick," he said. "You're Juniper's mother."

"No," she said. Her head shook. "Who am I really?"

Where did I learn how to fight like that? What am I capable of?

What have I done?

SIX

Owen listened as words poured, almost frantically, from Sara's lips, but he had no idea what to make of them. She was babbling and shaking. Meanwhile, they were standing on the icy street, with freezing-cold wind whipping at them and small ice pellets beginning to rain down around them.

"You're fine," Owen said. His hands rested lightly on her upper arms. "You're good. You're safe. Juniper and Lottie are safe. We're going to figure this out. That's all that matters right now."

He said the words with conviction, as if the sheer fact he willed them to be true would make them so.

"Owen, you don't understand," Sara said. "I need to know exactly who I am and what I've done. We can look in the outside world for who is behind all this, but what if it's me? What if all this is my fault?"

He stepped back and touched her cheek with his gloved fingertips.

"It's not your fault," Owen said. "I know what just happened was scary. But whatever your mind's all worked up about right now isn't important at this moment. All that matters is that you're safe."

He didn't mean to be dismissive. He was cold, she was upset and he was just trying to calm her down. But a quick and sudden flash of fire filled her eyes. She stepped back and away from his touch.

"No," she said. "You're wrong. That's not all that matters now. And as long as you keep thinking that way, this nightmare is never going to be over."

Tears filled her eyes, and he knew in that instant that something was wrong—something beyond the kidnapping she'd just survived.

Jess arrived moments later with two uniformed police officers, whom he recognized as local police. Sara joined them, and they took a few steps away from him and the vehicles. He couldn't hear the full description Sara gave them of her kidnapper—he had the distinct impression she didn't want him to. Then the police officers took off in the direction she'd pointed.

It was only then that the full strangeness of the situation hit him.

How had Sara escaped her kidnapper? Why was the kidnapper's gun in her vehicle?

Sara walked back to him. "I'm going to be a minute with Jess."

He noticed she didn't meet his eyes.

She walked back to join the others. He watched as Jess and Travis exchanged a few quick words, and then Travis sauntered over.

"So, you and I are going to go get the kids," Travis said. His tone was as casual as always while also giving no hint what he said was up for debate. "Sara's going to give Jess a full statement, and then they'll join us back at the house later."

"Why do I feel like I've been dismissed?" Owen said. "And like Sara's keeping stuff from me?"

"Probably because it's true," Travis said. "Whatever happened in that van, Sara's not ready to talk about all of it."

And Owen remembered that Travis didn't fully trust Sara.

A few minutes later, as Travis, Owen, Juniper and Lottie drove back into town, Travis said, "We've got to start thinking about what we're going to do if this drags on much longer. Obviously, we've been happy to have you, Sara and Juniper stay with us short-term. But Jess and I have agreed that if things aren't resolved in the next few hours or so, we're going to have to help her find a longer-term safe place to stay. We have a lot of friends in what I guess you'd call an unofficial witness protection network. They will keep her safe and off the grid without having to apply for official protection through law enforcement. Probably aiming to move her tomorrow."

Owen nodded. That was more than fair.

"In the meantime, I'm going to take all three of our kids to our friends Mack and Iris's home," Travis went on. "They're good people. The kids love spending time with them, and they'll keep them safe while this blows over. I'm sure they'd be happy to take Juniper too, but I assume you'd rather keep her with you."

Since the day he'd said goodbye to Sara and then been told she'd died, Juniper had never been out of his sight for more than a few hours at a time.

When he'd moved to Kilpatrick, he'd moved in to the tiny one-bedroom apartment over the town's only and derelict hardware store. Being mayor was a part-time job and one the town couldn't afford to pay much of a salary for, and as he'd always loved tools and making things, reopening the store had seemed like a natural fit. Juniper and he shared the bedroom, with her large wooden crib and his narrow single bed so close together he could almost reach out and touch her in his sleep. She had a second crib in his office at the back of the store with the quilt Sara had made her, and also a play mat on the floor in front of his desk. Not to mention another playpen behind the cash register in the store itself.

As his little girl grew more and more determined to stand and to crawl, he knew the days of keeping her that close while he worked were numbered.

And now that Sara was back, where would she want to live? In Ottawa? Back in Amish country?

How would they share custody?

If she went into hiding, would she want to take Juniper with her? How would that work?

"Thank you," Owen said. "I'll have to talk it over with Sara."

"Of course," Travis said.

"I'm really sorry," Owen added. "For what it's worth, when I called you from the snowmobile last night, I had no idea the chaos I was bringing to your door."

"Don't apologize," Travis said swiftly and firmly. "Also don't start going down the mental road of second guessing yourself either. You made the right decision when you called me, and I'm glad you did." Travis ran his hand over the back of his head. "I'm incredibly proud of the work Jess does taking down criminals, and I've actually recently started doing my own kind of secret thing working with citizen detectives too."

A secret thing. Right. Owen wanted to ask more but knew Travis would tell him if and when he was ready.

"I hope this is the last time any kind of danger ever comes near my home or my family," Travis said. Then his jaw set. "But also I've learned we don't always get to choose what arrives in our lives—only how we deal with it."

The friends lapsed into silence. The familiar buildings of Kilpatrick came into view. Owen wondered if he'd ever be able to explain to Sara the tug he felt inside him whenever he thought of this town that bore his family's name. Before his cousin had died in that hit-and-run, he'd told Owen he'd been approached by some big company wanting to buy out the town and turn it into a tourist trap. They'd rebrand it as a cutesy little winter-themed village, where tourists would flock to get the kitschy, faux-traditional holiday feeling. But Owen had traveled to enough places like that to know that with tourist traps, just a few steps away from the eight-dollar cups of fancy hot chocolate and twelve-dollar gingerbread, there were blocks upon blocks of boarded-up houses and people below the poverty line struggling to live. He'd told his cousin not to take it, his cousin had agreed and the company had never approached Owen or tried again.

But it stuck in Owen's mind as a reminder of just how fragile the financial state of the town his family had founded was. And even though in a few weeks Roger Wilson would be taking over as mayor, Owen was still dedicated to keeping the hardware store open.

He felt oddly responsible for Kilpatrick. He also loved his daughter more than words, and thankfully when he'd lost Sara, he'd found a way to care for Juniper while living in the very heart of the town he called home.

They picked up the kids and got to the farmhouse. Travis packed overnight bags for his kids and then took all three to stay with his friends, leaving Owen and Juniper alone in the house. The sky grew darker outside the windows, blocking out any last remaining glimpse of the pale sun he'd seen in the morning. The empty house loomed large around them, and small hail pellets clattered like pebbles against the windows.

He changed his little girl, fed her lunch and tried to nibble on some leftovers himself. By the time he heard a vehicle pull into the driveway, Owen was sitting cross-legged on the living room floor, with Juniper lying on a large blanket surrounded by stuffed toys and blocks.

The door opened, and Sara and Jess walked in, but as he went to stand, Sara waved a hand at him, gesturing for him to stay seated. She pulled off her boots and coat, gave Jess a quick hug and then sat down on the other side of the mat opposite Owen. Jess disappeared down the hallway. Sara sighed and leaned against the armchair. She looked exhausted.

Juniper looked up at her mother and babbled happily. The tiny baby waved her arms and legs, trying to launch herself toward her. And for the first time in a long time, Owen watched as a beautiful smile broke across Sara's face, illuminating her eyes, like the sun coming out at the end of a storm. Instinctively, Sara reached out for her, but Owen held up his hand and Sara sat back. Juniper dug one ankle into the floor and shoved herself forward an inch, then squealed with delight.

"She wants to do it herself," Owen explained. "She hasn't quite picked up the mechanics of crawling yet, but she seems determined to figure it out and make her own way of it."

They sat back and watched their daughter for a long moment.

"She's feisty," Sara said.

"Very," Owen laughed, "and determined. Like her mother."

Sara's blue eyes met his, and her smile faded.

"How'd everything go with Jess?" he asked.

"I gave her a full statement," Sara said, "and they're looking for..." As he watched, she caught whatever words she was about to say next and stopped herself from saying them. "They're looking for the person who kidnapped me."

The sniper's warning filled his mind.

Stop helping her and we'll leave you alone. Otherwise both you and your baby will die.

Had he been telling the truth? Were the criminals really only after Sara? Either way, he worried about what she'd do if he told her that.

Questions filled his mind, and he remembered how she'd stepped away from him to talk to Jess. What had happened with the kidnapper that she wasn't telling him about? But there was a look in her eyes—like doubt, or even fear—that made him wait.

"Jess told me that Travis is taking the kids to safety," Sara added. She took in a deep breath and let it out slowly, then she fixed her gaze back on the child currently propelling herself across the floor one determined kick at a time. "They said they're going to look into a safe house for me. I told her I'd rather return to Amish country."

"You're not safe there," he said.

"I was safe there for six months," she shot back, "before I went to the holiday market."

"You don't know that for certain."

"What do you know about me?" Sara asked. "I mean, really know about me?"

He bristled at her question, taking it as a challenge. But when he looked at her face, the look of worry in her eyes gave him pause.

"I'm guessing you don't mean stuff like that your favorite ice cream is rocky road," he said, "and that you're a dog person?"

An unexpected smile turned up one side of her lips.

"Nice try," she said. "I'm pretty sure I've always been a cat person."

To his surprise, he chuckled. He ran his hand over the back of his neck.

"You're right," he said. "You got me there. You've always been a cat person."

He closed his eyes and prayed for wisdom. Then he took a deep breath and let it out slowly.

"You were raised by a single mom," he said. "I never met her, and she died of cancer when you were twenty. But you always talked fondly of her."

"I remember her," Sara said and smiled sadly. "She didn't understand me, but she loved me."

Juniper finally reached her mother's toes and grabbed onto them. Sara looked down at her daughter, held out her fingers and let Juniper grab them. Slowly and care-fully, she helped Juniper pull herself up to standing.

"Have I always been strong and athletic, do you know?" she asked. Her eyes were still on Juniper. There was a tone to her voice he couldn't quite place.

"I think so," he said. "You joined the military re-serves at sixteen, and you used to get up every morning before the crack of dawn to hit the gym or the pool, or even just to run."

They'd decided to do a triathlon together early in their relationship, he remembered, but when he didn't keep up with his training, she ended up tackling it alone.

"Do you remember why?" she asked. "I mean, the reason I told you?"

Again, he couldn't understand where the questions were leading. Why was she asking about this now?

"Why you joined the military?" he asked.

She nodded.

"You cared about serving your country and liked a challenge. Also, money was tight, and the military paid your way through university."

Juniper stood unsteadily, holding on to Sara's fin-gers. She raised her legs one at a time and stomped the air, as if trying to figure out how they worked. It wouldn't be that long until she taught herself to walk.

"Where were you working when we met?" she asked.

"I was still in university," he admitted, "and work-ing for a landscaping and snowplowing company. I also did some construction and garage work."

He'd loved it, actually. So why had he pressured him-self to find the right university program?

"Where did we meet?" she asked.

"At a party," he said. "Your roommate Casey Brown invited me."

Sara's eyes widened. "You knew Casey?"

"You remember Casey?" Owen asked.

"No, not really," she said.

"Well, we were in the same class at law school," Owen said. "She invited me to a party, where I met you and we hit it off. I had no idea she'd thought she and I were on a date until she lost her temper with us both."

Sara's mouth gaped. She set Juniper back down gently to sitting. "Casey thought you were dating?"

Tension built at the back of his neck. They'd already had this argument, years ago, and he didn't have the patience to have it now.

"I'm the kind of person who makes decisions slowly," he said. "Like I might've I told you I'm wishy-washy."

He paused as the words left his mouth.

"Actually, scratch that," he corrected himself. "I'm the kind of person who makes decisions slowly after gathering a lot of information. And there's nothing wrong with that. It took me three tries at higher education before I realized it wasn't for me. So, when it came to relationships, I moved slowly and cautiously too. I had a couple of female acquaintances, including Casey, who hoped our relationship would lead to something more. Once you and I started dating, you made sure I called each and every one and told them I was taken, as well as posted it to social media. But I never led them on or even so much as hugged them."

That was the truth. And he was done apologizing for who he was.

"When I met you, everything was different," he said.

"There was this kind of light inside you—I don't know how else to put it. You had this drive. This dedication for everything that was good in life. We just started talking and talking, like there was nobody else in the room."

It had been one of the happiest moments of his life.

"I told you I'd tried a handful of different churches, but hadn't settled on one," he said. "So you invited me to come to yours the next day. I showed up the next morning, and you'd saved me a seat. We went out for coffee after the service. The next week, I showed up, and you'd saved me a seat again. This time we went out for lunch. The next week after church, we went for a long walk by the river and spent the whole day together. The following Friday, we went out for dinner, and I tried to kiss you good-night."

Heat rose to his face.

"What did I do?" Sara asked softly.

"You told me you weren't going to let me waste your time," he said. "Your job meant you could be transferred or moved at any time. You said you were looking for a man who wanted to marry you, build a life with you and start a family. And if I wasn't willing to try for something like that, then to step back now."

"How did you react?" she asked.

"I liked it," he said. "I thought we were good for each other. Fourteen months later we were married. I never actually proposed. You said you didn't need me to drop to my knees, take your hand and promise I'd be by your side forever. Because you knew we were right for each other, and knowing is enough."

Until somehow it wasn't, and the differences they'd

appreciated about each other at first ended up pushing them apart.

He ran his hand over his face as if wiping away memories.

"Why are you asking me about all this?" he asked. "What does it matter now?"

"The woman who kidnapped me said she was my old roommate, Casey."

"What?" Owen's voice rose sharply. Juniper started to fuss. Sara scooped her into her arms, then stood and began to pace.

Owen stood too.

"I don't know if it was really her," Sara said. "I didn't remember her. But she told me she was my old roommate, we met at the pool, she was a lawyer and she didn't like you."

"Well, all that's true about Casey," Owen said.

"She said I came to her for help. She said I stole some important military files for some very bad men and double-crossed them out of money."

She bounced and paced. It was disorienting to watch.

"What bad men?" he asked. "What was in the files?"

"I have no idea," Sara said. "She didn't tell me any of that. But there's more. I wrenched the gun from her hand, disarming her, and practically kicked her out of the vehicle."

"Right, you did what you had to in order to save your life."

She stopped suddenly and turned back. "No." Her voice was as sharp as a chef's knife. "You don't get it. I disarmed her one-handed while driving. I disarmed Coop yesterday. I leaped out of a second-story building without hesitation. I have skills, Owen. Terrifying skills. The kind a normal person shouldn't have."

Juniper started fussing again. Sara went back to pacing.

"You keep telling me I'm a good person, Owen," she said. "But what if you're wrong? What if I'm not? Who knows what I'm capable of?"

Footsteps sounded behind them. Sara turned and he followed her gaze. Jess was standing in the doorway holding a laptop.

"Sorry to interrupt," the detective said. "But I need to show you something." She searched their faces for a moment as if checking for silent approval. Then she turned the laptop around. Casey's smiling face filled the screen in what looked like a professional picture he guessed she'd pulled from a company website. "Is this the woman who kidnapped you?"

Sara shook her head. "No."

Owen let out a long breath and thanked God.

"That's Casey Brown," he said. "So that's not who kidnapped you."

As he watched, relief coursed over Sara's form. But Jess's face was grim.

"How about her?" Jess asked and pulled up a different picture of a woman several years older with a fake smile and obnoxiously pink blazer. "We traced the gun in the SUV, and she was listed as the owner."

Owen watched as Sara's body stiffened.

"It's her," Sara said.

"She's an interior decorator from Montreal named Delia Karnel," Jess said and blew out a long breath. "I don't know how she's possibly connected. Casey quit her job around the time Sara disappeared and seemingly dropped off the map. And I'm at a loss."

Then Jess glanced at Owen. "Travis said he told you that he was involved in an anonymous citizen investigation group?"

Owen nodded.

"Well," Jess said, "I think it's time we let you in."

About an hour and a half later, Sara, Owen, Travis and Jess sat around the kitchen table. This time the mood and tone were completely different from the light, boisterous and joyful air that had filled the room earlier. Hail beat hard against the darkened window.

Sara sat beside Jess at one end of the table, with Jess's laptop open in front of them. On the other side of the table sat Owen and Travis in front of Travis's laptop. Juniper sat on the table between them in her car seat, with her back to the window and her eyes wide as she happily batted at the crinkly butterfly and squeaky ladybug that hung in front of her. On the counter were two large pizzas that Travis had brought back for them after dropping their kids off at their friends' house, and even though they'd each nibbled at a piece or two, none of them had much of an appetite.

Jess prayed softly, and then she opened the video chat. Sara watched the screen, not knowing what to expect. One by one, small video chat boxes filled the screen, including one of Travis and Owen sitting together in front of the laptop across the table from them.

"Hey, everyone," Travis said. He waved in greeting. "These are the friends we messaged you about, Owen and Sara. Owen and Sara, welcome to the Joe and Jane

Doe Justice Group. For simplicity, we tend to just go by the JJs."

There were about a dozen people, ranging in age between twenty and eighty. There were men and women, people dressed casually and those in work clothes, sitting in front of windows that included both wild snowstorms and sunny skies. Oddly, something about it reminded her of the Amish meeting house. Then she realized one was Anne, the doctor.

"The JJs have been my passion project for the past year," Travis explained, "after our friend Seth helped Jess on a major serial-killer cold case that was over twenty years old. He's one of the best hackers in the world, and thankfully is on our side catching killers."

On the screen, a man with disheveled blond hair, sitting at what looked like a cluttered desk, raised a hand and said, "Hello."

He was the only one whose on screen display didn't list a name, but she guessed that was Seth.

"There are thousands of missing people and cold cases across North America," Travis went on, "and a lot of people needing justice, peace and closure. But police have limited resources and can't investigate things outside their jurisdictions. That's where we come in. We're a group of concerned citizen investigators—including retired law enforcement, students, lawyers, homemakers, you name it—who pool our resources to crowdsource information and pass it on to the right people in law enforcement who can make a difference. Whether it's searching social media or library archives or ancestry websites or making phone calls and sending emails."

"And we do it all anonymously," chipped in an elderly man in a tweed jacket. His video screen box identified him as Bert. "For our own safety and the safety of those involved."

Heads nodded.

"Well said," Travis agreed. "Now, you should all have the basic notes on the case I sent through an encrypted message. Let's start by going through the characters we're dealing with, starting with Officers Jimmy Beau and Tony Coop."

And for the first time, Sara felt a small glimmer of hope that they might finally get answers.

"I can confirm that neither officer has left the police department all day," Bert said. There was a certainty to his voice that made her wonder if he had a contact on the inside or had been literally parked across the street from the police station all day watching the doors. "I expect they'll be suspended without pay, but they won't be held overnight."

"I've done a detailed search through their criminal records," the hacker named Seth said. "Coop's record is pretty clean, but Beau has a couple of minor assault charges. Certainly nothing that would even begin to explain how they got caught up in this."

"I've combed through every scintilla of data on their social media, and there's nothing that links the two men," a woman named Tessa chimed in. She had beautifully tousled shoulder-length curls and seemed to be sitting in some kind of cabin. "They didn't grow up in the same town, their kids aren't at the same school, their kids don't go to the same gym, they have no friends in common. They've never even worked on a case together. There's nothing that links them."

"Except for the fact they apparently got up extremely early yesterday morning, robbed an Amish farmhouse and then set it on fire. That's an eight-hour drive from their homes, then spent all day trying to track down and kidnap someone together," Seth said dryly.

"How about Delia Karnel?" Travis asked.

"Again, no known connection between her and the other two men," Tessa stated.

"But a much more interesting record," Seth cut in. "She's had the police called on her plenty of times, for public intoxication, getting into fights, throwing fits in stores or restaurants when she doesn't get her way."

"A lot of overly emotional social media posts," Tessa added. "She's the kind of dramatic person who's always up for a fight. Also, based on the way she spends money, I expect she's got financial problems."

"That I can confirm," Seth chimed in. "She has a lot of consumer debt."

"But again, nothing to explain why she'd kidnap Sara?" Travis asked.

There was a long pause as heads shook. Nobody had anything.

"What about Casey?" Sara asked. "Have you turned up anything on her?"

Tessa's eyebrow quirked. "No, sorry," she said. "Nothing yet. But I'll dig deeper."

"Thank you," Sara said.

"Anything on my dentist, Dr. Freck?" Owen asked.

"Another bad credit score," Seth said. "He put in a couple of failed applications for a second mortgage on his house. Maybe he was vulnerable to blackmail."

"Any hunches about his cause of death, Anne?" Travis asked.

The doctor ran both hands through her hair then rested her elbows on the table.

"Obviously, I don't have access to a toxicology report or medical examiner's report," Anne said. "But you can tell a lot from a body and the scene. Based on the pictures you sent and the description you gave me, it looks like a painkiller overdose. I don't know if it was intentional though. Due to his age, there could've been health complications or memory issues. But either way, he fell asleep at his desk and never woke up."

Owen let out a long breath, and she suspected he was thankful the dentist hadn't suffered. She reached for his hand across the table, but when he didn't take it, she pulled back.

"So, we're working from the hypothesis that our criminal shot up the dentist's office in order to obscure the fact the Dr. Freck was poisoned," Bert said. "What we don't know if he deliberately waited until someone was there to fire. Or if Owen showing up right before the office opened was an unfortunate coincidence."

"I should've told people this earlier," Owen said, "but the sniper said something to me in the woods before he got away."

Travis inhaled sharply. Sara felt her eyes widen.

The sniper had spoken to him? And he'd never told her?

"He told me that he was going to spare my life because he was only after Sara," Owen continued, "and that if I didn't stop helping her, he'd kill both me and our daughter."

"You should've told me!" Sara's voice rose.

Owen's eyes met his across the tables.

"And if I had, then what?" he shot back. "You'd have run? The point is we can't trust anything this guy says. He fired a gun into the dentist's office, when I was standing there. Did he deliberately miss me? Was he using me to set up his alibi? I don't know!"

Sara swallowed a hard breath. Delia had told her that it was her fault all this had happened, and now she knew that the sniper had told Owen the same.

"Okay," Travis said. "Big-picture story time."

He waved his hands through the air as if unfurling an invisible map.

"Sara gets her hands on something that somebody wants," Travis said. "Somebody else shoots her in an attempt to get it. Sara gets away, and somebody fakes her death. Maybe the person who shot her was hired by someone, and when she got away, he got creative because he wanted the big baddy to think he'd finished the job. He somehow gets our elderly dentist to confirm it's Sara via dental records. Six months later, the big baddy gets wind of where Sara is and sends Coop and Beau to retrieve what she stole—"

"Oh!" Tessa interjected. "Her picture appeared in a newspaper article about the local holiday fair. Not her name, but you can see her face."

"That would do it," Travis said with a sigh. "So Coop and Beau try to retrieve whatever Sara has. She gets away. They get drawn up. Big baddy gets the dentist to destroy the dental records in case someone comes to check them and sends Delia to get Sara. Any questions?"

"Should we look into the funeral home director who buried this fake Sara?" Tessa asked.

"You can," Owen said. "But I don't see what role he'd have played. He's a young guy named Derek Pond, inherited the business from his father, Dan."

There was another pause. Then a plump woman with long blond hair raised her hand. Her chat box identified her as Vanessa.

"What did you have on you when you were found, Sara?" Vanessa asked. "Memory sticks are small. Memory cards are even smaller. Is it possible you had the files on you and didn't realize it?"

Sara closed her eyes and thought.

"I was wearing blue jeans, a T-shirt, a sweatshirt and sneakers," she said. "They were all basically destroyed. I don't think I had anything else on me."

Then a thought struck her. Had she sewn the memory device into the seams of her clothes?

"And your wedding ring," Owen said.

"Right."

Funny, she was so used to having it on her person that it felt like a part of her. Slowly, she reached around behind her neck and unclasped the chain, her chest feeling oddly empty without the weight of the ring resting there. She passed the ring to Jess, who took a long look and then passed it across the table to Travis, who looked at it too, as did Owen. Then he passed it back to Sara, who held it out to the screen. But Owen was convinced the ring was the same as when he'd slid it on her finger on their wedding day. It didn't seem to have been tampered with. And nobody thought it contained anything fishy.

"How do we contact the Amish couple who found

FREE BOOKS GIVEAWAY

GET UP TO FOUR FREE BOOKS & TWO FREE GIFTS WORTH OVER $20!

We pay for everything!

YOU pick your books –
WE pay for everything.

You get up to FOUR New Books and TWOMystery Gifts...absolutely FREE!

Dear Reader,

I am writing to announce the launch of a huge **FREE BOOKS GIVEAWAY**... and to let you know that YOU are entitled to choose up to FOUR fantastic books that WE pay for.

Try **Love Inspired® Romance Larger-Print** books and fall in love with inspirational romances that take you on an uplifting journey of faith, forgiveness and hope.

Try **Love Inspired® Suspense Larger-Print** books where courage and optimism unite in stories of faith and love in the face of danger.

Or TRY BOTH!

In return, we ask just one favor: Would you please participate in our brief Reader Survey? We'd love to hear from you.

This FREE BOOKS GIVEAWAY means that your introductory shipment is completely free, <u>even the shipping</u>! If you decide to continue, you can look forward to curated monthly shipments of brand-new books from your selected series, always at a discount off the cover price! <u>Plus you can cancel any time</u>. Who could pass up a deal like that?

Sincerely

Pam Powers

Pam Powers
For Harlequin Reader Service

Complete the survey below and return it today to receive up to 4 FREE BOOKS and FREE GIFTS guaranteed!

FREE BOOKS GIVEAWAY
Reader Survey

1	**2**	**3**
Do you prefer books which reflect Christian values?	Do you share your favorite books with friends?	Do you often choose to read instead of watching TV?
◯ YES ◯ NO	◯ YES ◯ NO	◯ YES ◯ NO

YES! Please send me my Free Rewards, consisting of **2 Free Books from each series I select** and **Free Mystery Gifts**. I understand that I am under no obligation to buy anything, no purchase necessary see terms and conditions for details.

❑ **Love Inspired® Romance Larger-Print** (122/322 IDL GRP7)
❑ **Love Inspired® Suspense Larger-Print** (107/307 IDL GRP7)
❑ **Try Both** (122/322 & 107/307 IDL GRQK)

FIRST NAME

LAST NAME

ADDRESS

APT.#

CITY

STATE/PROV.

ZIP/POSTAL CODE

EMAIL ❑ Please check this box if you would like to receive newsletters and promotional emails from Harlequin Enterprises ULC and its affiliates. You can unsubscribe anytime.

her?" Vanessa asked. "Might they have found something on her and not realized the importance of it?"

"I have no way to contact them while they're traveling," Sara said. "They don't even know about the home invasion or the house fire. Once they've arrived at their destination, they'll call the phone box in their community and let people know they arrived safely. Then someone will tell them what happened."

Sara wished she could be there when the phone rang in the community phone booth to talk to them.

"How bad was the fire," Tessa asked. "Did it burn the entire house down? It was pretty snowy yesterday, and the fire might not have spread to the entire house. Maybe part of it is still standing."

Bert cleared his throat.

"Clearly somebody needs to hack into Sara's secret military records," Bert said. "She may have stolen national secrets and tried to sell them to terrorists or mercenaries. But it appears nobody who's capable of doing that is willing to do it."

An odd and uncomfortable silence fell around the group.

"Just throwing this out there," Owen said, breaking the silence, "but if we had a DNA sample of whoever was buried in Sara's grave, we'd be able to figure out who she is, right?"

Heads nodded enthusiastically.

"I can get you a DNA match in less than twenty-four hours," Anne said.

"And if there are no matches in the system, we can compare them to publicly available DNA records, like ancestry websites," Tessa added, "then contact those people and see if they know who she is. We've done it before."

"Lawyer here," a handsome man with dark stubble named Rowan spoke up. "Legally exhuming a body is tricky and can take months. You'd need permission from the local authority and have to go before a judge."

A low groan spread around the group.

"On the other hand," Rowan added, "your situation is a bit unique. You're the mayor, right?"

"For a few more weeks," Owen said.

"Right, so you're the top authority in town," Rowan said. "Plus the grave is technically on your land. So, while it's still not legal, if you were caught, you'd probably be looking at a misdemeanor. Maybe a fine."

She watched as the corner of Owen's lips quirked on one side and his forehead wrinkled.

He couldn't actually be considering digging up the grave?

"I appreciate what everyone's doing," Sara said. "But I don't want to do anything criminal, and that includes digging up a grave."

"You seem to be forgetting the fact you might've already done something criminal," Bert said.

"No, believe me, I haven't," Sara said firmly. "I know you might not all respect my faith. But I have to believe there's a way to solve this while still being true to who I am and what I believe."

An awkward silence fell around the group again just like it had when Bert had mentioned getting into the military files. Seth raised his hand.

"Hey," he said, "would it be okay if I talk to Sara off the group video for a minute? I just wanna go over a couple things that she might not want to discuss in the group."

Sara glanced at Owen. He shrugged.

"Sure," she said.

Jess pushed a button, and all the boxes disappeared but Seth's. Then Jess went around to the other side of the table and joined Travis and Owen. Sara carried the laptop into the living room, set it down on the coffee table, then sat on the couch. When he'd just been in a small box, something about his scruffy hair and way of slouching in his chair made Sara think Seth was in his twenties. Now she could see he was a decade or two older than that.

"The reason everyone had a weird reaction when Bert suggested I hack into your military files is because hacking into the military used to be my deal," Seth said. "Growing up, my dad was in the army, and he was a nasty piece of work. I got really jaded and started hacking things and leaking them. I started with the military and then expanded to anyone I felt like targeting. I told myself I was just hacking criminals, like a digital Robin Hood. But law enforcement didn't always see it that way, and I ended up with a criminal record. Then I went after the wrong guy, got taken hostage and ended up in witness protection. That's how I met Jess and Travis and some of their friends."

"Wow," Sara said.

"Yeah. And that's the short version. See, they might talk about me as some great hero. But to me, I'm still the guy who broke the law and made some big mistakes. I've been working at turning my life around, and that includes not doing anything illegal. There's no way to hack into your military files without breaking the law. Now, if you believe that's the only way to save your life and save your baby's life, then let me know. But until then, I'm gonna try to find a way to do it legally. I just wanted you to know that you and I were on the same page about that."

"Thank you," she said. "I hope it won't come to that."

"Me too," he said. "If that's what has to happen, I'm on it. Until then, I'll work double time to find everything and anything I can legally."

She took a deep breath.

"Delia told me I had papers drawn up trying to take Juniper away from Owen and to keep him from contacting me," she said. And for some reason, she still hadn't told Owen yet. She couldn't hurt him like that. Not until she knew for herself if they were real. "Can you find out if that's true? And keep it on the down low?"

He nodded. "Will do." He rattled off his cell phone number and told her to call him anytime. Then he added, "And if it turns out you are a criminal and did steal and try to sell military files, you're not alone. And you can rebuild your life. I promise you that."

The window closed, leaving her alone with a blank screen.

Sara slid to her knees, folded her hands on the table and prayed.

Almighty God, I feel so lost and confused right now. Like I don't know who I am anymore. For the last few months, I've been living the plain *way of life, following You the best I can. Now I'm in a totally different world, and I might have been a horrible person in my past. You are the only one Who has always been there.*

You've always known me and always loved me. Please guide my steps. Help me trust You now.

Voices fell silent in the kitchen. She opened her eyes to see Owen standing in the doorway. His face was calm, his eyes unreadable.

"I've got to run to my hardware store to get some supplies," Owen said. "I've decided I'm going to wait until dark, and then I'm going to dig up the grave."

SEVEN

The door chimes jangled as Owen pushed the front door open and stepped inside the Kilpatrick Hardware Store. The air was soft and dark. He breathed deeply, letting the familiar smell of wood fill his lungs. Then he walked in, flipping on the lights as he went.

"Welcome to my store," Owen said.

Sara followed him inside. She'd changed into a long dark dress and simple bonnet. A long piece of cloth wrapped around her torso and shoulders, holding Juniper to her chest.

He closed the door behind them, locked it and double-checked the blinds were thoroughly closed. He hadn't known what to think when she'd asked if she could go with him to the hardware store to pick up the tools they'd need for digging up the grave. He half suspected she'd come along because she wanted to talk him out of what he was planning. But now that they were here, she seemed genuinely interested in seeing his business. And to be honest, he was thankful for the opportunity to show her what he'd built.

Travis sat in his truck on the other side of the street,

casually keeping watch, and Jess was on the top floor of Tatlow's bookstore getting an aerial view. All four of them were connected by hidden walkie-talkies and could talk to each other at the touch of a button. And yet, none of that did anything to ease the butterflies in Owen's stomach at realizing he was alone with Sara inside his store.

"When my cousin died, I discovered that a lot of the stores I remembered had closed," he said, "and the residents that did remain were deeply in debt to various unscrupulous loan institutions. In fact, a few months earlier, some tacky real estate company had tried to buy all the stores on Main Street and turn this into some perpetual winter-fair tourist trap."

Which reminded him, the calls on his phone had been piling up from residents wanting to suggest more elaborate things they could add to next month's fair.

He watched as Sara walked through the store and took it all in—the meticulous wall of tools, the small plastic drawers filled with every kind of nut, bolt and screw that anyone could need, the racks of safety gear and the spinning shelf of DIY books.

"This place is amazing," Sara said. Awe filled her voice.

Pride swelled in his chest.

"You should've seen the wreck the place was in," he said. "There were broken and dusty shelves filled with the kind of cheap stuff you'd find in the bottom of the bin at a dollar store. Nothing people could actually use. Nothing of value. But something inside me was just drawn to this place. I figured if the town was going to rebuild itself, what it needed was a good hardware store.

I wanted to give people a fighting chance, and you can't build anything without the right tools."

She stopped in front of the huge bulletin board beside the cash register. Brightly colored cards filled every corner, advertising for handyman and construction services of every kind, along with people advertising their ability to bake cakes, babysit, unclog toilets, walk dogs, shovel snow and mow lawns. Her eyes widened.

"This is incredible," she said. "I'm guessing this was all your idea?"

"Well, I figured this town was full of people who had skills they could share with those who needed them," he said. "And I was going to do my best to bring them together. People care about this town. And I wanted to help empower them to fix it."

A chorus of loud knocking sounded on the store's front door. They both jumped. Instinctively, he reached for Sara and slid a protective arm around her waist. With the other hand, he pressed the button on his walkie-talkie.

"Who's there?" he asked.

"Just a couple of the town busybodies," Travis said. Owen could practically hear him rolling his eyes. "We've got Ruby the florist and Dolores, who keeps trying to make my wife buy shawls."

"He means Dorothy," Owen whispered to Sara with a wry smile, "who owns the fashion boutique across from Roger Wilson's law firm."

Travis was excellent at a great many things, but general people skills was definitely not one of them.

"Ruby and Dorothy are both on the winter fair committee," Owen said to the group. "They've been trying to reach me nonstop since yesterday with all kinds of weird and wonderful ideas for making this year's fair even more fabulous."

Travis snorted.

"What kind of ideas?" Sara asked.

"A giant waterfall made entirely of lights and a bouncy house obstacle course, for starters," Owen said. "But I know they have other ideas too. Sounds like that party Roger threw at his law firm the other night turned into a pretty major brainstorming session."

And in a few weeks, the bombastic lawyer would be in charge of the town budget. But for now, all the boring and responsible decisions still rested on Owen's shoulders.

The knocking grew louder. He guessed they'd seen his truck in the parking lot. Juniper began to fuss; she probably wanted out of her chest sling.

"Why don't you go talk to them," Sara said. "I'll take Juniper into the back and let her stretch out and play for a bit. We've got Travis and Jess watching our backs."

"Okay," he said. The fact the winter fair was the last thing on his mind right now didn't mean it wasn't important to the community. He pointed to the open door of his office behind the counter. Inside was Juniper's crib, with the beautiful quilt of butterflies and wildflowers Sara had made for her draped over a rail. "You've got everything you'll need for her in my office—toys, blankets, diapers, snacks, you name it. I'll give you a shout and come get you when I'm done. And of course, feel free to listen in on the walkie."

He waited until Sara and Juniper went into his office and closed the door. Then he walked back through

the hardware store toward the incessant banging, wondering just how long they'd stand out there and wait
if he didn't answer the door. He took a deep breath,
prayed for patience and then smiled, reminding himself that these people didn't know—couldn't possibly
know—about everything else going on in his life. Then
he opened the door.

"Ruby! Dorothy! Hi!" he said. He positioned himself in the doorway, blocking the entrance to the store,
and talked to them under the front awning, where they
were sheltered from the mix of snow and hail that was
falling. "Sorry I haven't returned your calls yet. I've
had some personal stuff to deal with."

Both women started talking at once, their voices
blending together in harmony as they filled him in on
all the creative but expensive-sounding ideas that had
apparently been brainstormed at the party the night before and that they were certain could put the town on
the map. There was talk of decorating each building on
Main Street with thousands of tiny lights that would
blink in sync to music, turning each shop and store
into an individually playable instrument in a grand or-
chestra of light. There was talk of bringing in a world-
renowned artist to carve ice sculptures and another to
break the record for the largest fireworks display. Before
they'd even begun to give up steam, the man who owned
the town bakery drove by, stopped his car, got out and
jumped in on the conversation, concerned that his idea
of holding a cupcake competition with renowned bak-
ers from across the country hadn't been properly heard.

It was a deluge after that, person after person ap-
pearing on the street and crowding under the awning

to escape the winter weather and say their two cents. One resident wanted a gourmet hot chocolate stand, and another wanted to bring lumberjacks in from across the country for a skills competition. But encouragingly, a couple asked about the budget too. Owen listened, took it all in with a smile and made sure everyone felt heard without making any commitments or promises he didn't know he'd be able to keep.

He liked this part of the job of being mayor. Truth was he'd miss it once he handed the reins over to Roger. Eventually, almost half an hour later, his impromptu visitors began to leave with smiles on their faces, having said their piece.

He turned and stepped back inside the store.

"Sorry about that," he said quietly into his walkie-talkie. "That took a bit longer than I expected."

"You're really good at that," Sara said. "I'm impressed."

Something filled her voice that he hadn't heard in a long time—admiration.

His breath caught in his chest. It wasn't like she'd never complimented him in the past. But something was different this time. He believed her. This time he knew deep inside that she was impressed by him.

Maybe she'd always meant it, just as deeply and sincerely as she did now, but he didn't believe in himself enough to hear it.

He was shutting the front door when a large hand in a leather glove that made him think of a bear's paw shot into the gap and stopped him.

"Sorry, we're closed," Owen said automatically.

"You sure?" a deep voice boomed. "Looked to me like you were hosting a porch party."

The mayor-elect was standing on his front step. Roger was a large man, at least six-five he guessed, with a width and bulk equally as imposing as his height and a thick mane of silver curls.

Owen ran a hand over his beard.

"I dropped by the store for a few minutes," he said, "and suddenly there was a whole bunch of people descending to tell me all about the amazing ideas you guys brainstormed last night at your party."

Roger laughed. "Yeah, I don't know what got into them, but I do love the zeal and enthusiasm of this place."

The lawyer was a big-city man with a permanent home in Toronto and a lavish summer cottage on a private lake near Kilpatrick and was usually only in town a few weeks a year. He'd opened a small part-time law practice in town that covered real estate and business law, mostly providing legal work for the kind of people who bought and sold cottages like his. When Owen had announced he would be stepping down as interim mayor at the winter fair, he hadn't expected Roger to be the only one to volunteer to take the job. But the man definitely had the kind of dynamic presence people were looking for in a mayor and shared their drive to put the town on the map. Roger dropped a heavy hand onto Owen's shoulder.

"I don't want to overstep," Roger said. "But I also have a small loan company in the city. Nothing big. Just select loans to people I trust. I wanted to drop by to offer to come in with a loan to help the city pay for the winter fair. It's clear people in this town have big dreams, and as my inauguration is going to be part of it, I want to chip in."

Owen stepped backward from the man's hand. Roger was presenting it as an offer, but something about the size of his smile made it feel more like a sales pitch.

"I appreciate the offer," Owen said, "but I can't justify adding to our debt on my way out the door."

"Look, I get it," Roger said. He raised his hands palms up. "I appreciate a good balanced budget as much as the next guy. I have a couple of different business irons in the fire actually, and they're all ticking away making money for me. I just know that our beloved town is cash-strapped and wanted to help you go out with a bang."

In other words, he wanted to make sure his own inauguration was as splashy as possible, with as many twinkling lights, ice displays and hot chocolate fountains as possible.

"Thanks," Owen said and nodded noncommittally. "I'll think about it."

The men shook hands, then Owen stepped back through the door and locked it behind him. He walked through the silent store. Gentle yellow light shone from inside his office. He pushed the door open. Juniper was playing on the quilt on the floor and gurgled in greeting. Sara was sitting behind his desk. She looked up, worry filling her eyes.

"What's wrong?" Owen asked. He rushed to her side before she could stand. He touched her arm. "What happened?"

"Nothing," Sara said. She shook her head. "I was just looking at your town budgets and spreadsheets. I hope you don't mind. They were just lying out here on the desk."

He followed her gaze to the printouts that covered the surface around his computer. Then he pulled up a chair and collapsed into it. Yeah, they would be enough to put worry in anyone's eyes.

"I heard you talking to all those people about their ideas," she said.

"And realized there's no money for any of it?" he asked, finishing the thought for her.

"Yeah," she said.

"I know." He nodded slowly. "Thing is, it didn't use to be that way. The town used to make enough money to cover expenses, and the winter fair was just a bonus. But now people treat it almost like a slot machine. They pour money into it, hoping it'll pay off."

He shrugged and then winced as the tension in his neck pinched between his shoulders. Silently, Sara got out of her chair and stood behind him. Her fingers ran along the side of his neck and pressed into the knots at the base of his skull, and for the first time in longer than he could remember, he felt his shoulders begin to relax.

"I wish I'd had the courage to run against Roger for mayor," he said. "But I may not have won. He's all pizazz, and I can't compete with that. But I like being mayor. I think I'm good at it."

Her strong yet tender touch stopped, as if Sara had caught herself and realized what she was doing. But he reached for her hands, and she let him take them—neither of them pulled away.

"I guess I needed to be in this job for a while before I got my head around it and realized how much it meant to me," he added, "and by the time it truly sank in, it was too late."

"There's nothing wrong with taking things slowly," she said.

If only she'd said those words when they'd been rushing into marriage and hurrying down the aisle to the altar. Maybe if they'd taken more time to fall in love, they wouldn't have fallen out of it again. Maybe their relationship wouldn't have ended.

Maybe Sara would've never been shot, and this whole mess would've never happened.

He stood up slowly. Her hand slipped from his, but she didn't step back. He turned and they stood there for a long moment, face-to-face, with his office chair wedged in between them. He wanted to wrap his arms around her and kiss her lips. He wanted to promise her they'd fall in love again and that this time their relationship would be different.

Instead, he stepped back and slipped around the side of the desk toward Juniper.

"Are we going to talk about my plan to dig up the grave?" he asked.

She frowned. "I don't like it. It feels wrong. And the fact you can make the argument it's not totally illegal still doesn't make it the right thing."

"But the sooner we figure out who's buried in your grave, the sooner we get justice for her," he said. "And the faster this whole thing gets wrapped up, and you can get back to your Amish way of life, if that's what you really want."

He wasn't quite sure why he'd thrown that last part out, or if he'd intended it to sound that much like a challenge or even a gauntlet thrown. But now that the words were said, an agonizing part of him wanted to hear her disagree with them.

Instead, she nodded. "You're right. Even though I don't agree with your methods."

And just like that, the tension was back in his neck.

He left her to play with Juniper as he gathered supplies. When they left, the street was empty and both Travis and Jess gave the all clear. They all went back to the Tatlows' farmhouse, where the day stretched out in long, quiet hours, as he tried and failed at napping, eating something, reading a book and not thinking about the future.

Anne arrived again with the kit they'd use to collect the DNA sample and offered to stay with Juniper while the others went to the grave. Owen put Juniper to bed, and they waited as the sun set and the night drew on, until shortly after two o'clock in the morning, when the snow stopped falling.

Owen and Sara drove together in his truck, while Travis and Jess went in their vehicle. They drove in silence. He glanced up at the dark clouds that covered the stars. The plan was as simple and precise as Owen could make it. He'd use a ground-penetrating radar device, or GPR, to scan the area beneath the snow to identify the exact location of the body. Then they'd dig straight down, creating as small a hole as possible and piling the dirt carefully on a tarp, until they reached the coffin. He'd crack open the coffin with a crowbar, gently clip off one of her fingernails for Anne to get tested, then close it back up with epoxy, shovel the dirt back in and then bury it with snow. The impending flurries would do the rest.

That was the plan as he'd explained it to Sara. There

was one other element he'd decided to keep from her—the small handgun he had tucked in a holster on his ankle. Carrying a concealed weapon wasn't strictly legal in Canada. Even if it were, he was sure Sara wouldn't like it. But just because she'd embraced a pacifist way of life as part of her newfound Amish faith, that didn't relieve him of his responsibility to protect his family. Right?

Truth was, his conscience was clear about arming himself. Not so much about not telling Sara about it.

"Here, take my phone," Owen said. He reached into his pocket and handed it to her across the front seat. "If anything happens, it's got all the numbers you need programmed in it—Anne, Travis, Jess and even their hacker friend, Seth."

"Thank you," she said. She took it from his hands and slipped it in the pocket of her coat.

"You don't have to do this if you don't want to," Owen said. "You're welcome to stay home with Anne and Juniper and try to get some sleep."

"I know," Sara said. "But even though I don't like this plan, I still feel like I need to help this woman in my grave, whoever she is. In her own way, she's lost, like I was. There are people who love her who don't know where she is or what happened to her." Her chin rose. "She died because of me, and I have a responsibility to help her."

He glanced at her. Lights and shadows fell over the lines of her face. Somehow she was even more beautiful than he'd remembered, but closed off too. Like there was a part of her she was afraid of letting him see.

He parked the truck on the service road, and they walked up the hill together toward the grave.

God, help us get the answers we need tonight to end this whole thing and get justice.

He activated the GPR and started to scan the ground, noting the bodies buried underground as they went. They reached the grave where he'd been reunited with Sara less than two days earlier, and they joined Travis and Jess, bundled up against the cold.

Travis laid the tarp out beside the grave, ready to dig. Owen scanned the ground for the coffin. He paused and searched it again.

Then he froze.

"Guys," Owen said. "Something's very wrong. I found the coffin. But it's empty. There's no body buried in Sara's grave."

Sara's mind went blank. Her grave was empty?

Travis was the one who found his voice first. "What do you mean it's empty? How is that possible?"

"I don't know," Owen said. "Look for yourself!"

Sara watched as he held the device up for them all to see. He swung it past other graves slowly before settling on Sara's.

"See what I'm saying?" Owen said. "You can see that someone's been laid to rest in every other spot. But not this one." He pointed down to Sara's grave, and his voice rose. "Her coffin is empty."

"Are we sure there was even a body to begin with?" Sara asked.

"Yes," Jess said. "I know cops who were at the scene,

and I saw the crime scene photos myself. Somebody was definitely found dead in your car."

"And now their body is missing," Owen said.

He ran his hand over his head. Sara could feel her own heart beating so hard it seemed to block out all other sounds. She felt dizzy. She wanted to reach for Owen, feel his arms around her and rest in his strength. Instead, she walked over to a nearby clump of trees and leaned against the closest one.

So, somebody had been killed in her place, identified as her and then disappeared. Where did they go? What did this even mean?

Help us, Lord. I feel more lost right now than ever.

"Hey!" An unfamiliar male voice filled the air, punctuated by large sweeps of a flashlight. Someone was running toward them across the snow. "What are you doing? Get away from there! I've got a gun, and I'm not afraid to use it."

Instinctively, Sara ducked behind the tree and watched as the running man grew closer. Travis turned the full beam of his flashlight onto the man's face. He was in his early twenties with panicked eyes and a mop of curly dark hair sticking out from under a winter cap that looked more fashionable than functional. A small handgun shook in his hands.

"Okay now, what's this?" Owen said. She watched Owen start to reach for something she couldn't see down by his ankle. Then he straightened up again, as if thinking twice about what he was going to do. Owen took a deep breath, and she watched as courage filled his form. Then he raised his voice cheerfully and stretched out his hand toward the approaching figure, as if he hadn't even noticed the gun. "Derek? Derek Pond? Is that you?"

Sara racked her brain to remember where she'd heard the name. Derek Pond was the young funeral director who'd inherited the funeral home from his father.

"What are you doing out here in the middle of the night?" Owen asked the question she was thinking.

"I… I… You…you guys are trying to rob a grave!" Derek stammered for words.

What? How did he know that? Why was he even here?

But despite both the danger and ridiculousness of the situation, Owen wasn't giving an inch.

"It's Mayor Kilpatrick," Owen said. He pulled himself up to his full height, and an authority she'd never seen in him before filled his frame. "And why would you possibly think that?"

"I…it doesn't matter," Derek said.

His teeth were chattering. She couldn't tell if it was from the cold or fear. But she knew something about the whole scene was wrong. This was all far too convenient.

"What are you even doing out here?" Owen asked.

"I… I got a call from somebody telling me there were grave robbers?"

"A call?" Owen said. "From who?"

"I don't know."

Owen chuckled softly, and something about it sent a chill down her spine.

"Listen," Owen said and took a step closer to the young man. "You know and I know that there's no body in this grave right here. You lied to me and everyone and buried an empty casket in the ground."

Sara watched as the color drained from Derek's face.

"Now, I don't need to explain to you why I'm here in the middle of the night trying to figure out what happened to the body in my wife's grave. And to be honest, I didn't involve you in whatever's going on because I didn't think you were involved. But now you're telling me that not only did you commit a crime, you got a mysterious phone call sending you here, and on top of that, Dr. Freck is dead. So how about you stop waving that gun around before you shoot your own toe off and tell me what's really going on?"

Derek hesitated, and Sara held her breath.

"The day before your wife's funeral, I got a call telling me to cremate her body," Derek said. "They told me if I did, they'd give me money to pay off my student loans. A lot of money."

Another anonymous call from an unknown source.

"Really?" Owen asked incredulously. "You really don't know who called?"

"It was a cop, okay?" Derek said. "Like a government one. They said she was an intelligence asset, and I'd be helping my country."

A red dot of light darted from the tree line like an insect and alighted on Derek's chest.

"Shooter!" Owen shouted.

Owen turned and ran for Sara, just as a shot fired, catching Derek in the chest and sending him flying back. Travis and Jess leaped for the young man as he fell. Owen caught Sara protectively in his arms and brought her down to the ground, shielding her with his body. A second shot flew from the trees.

"It was a setup," Owen said. "Somebody sent Derek out here to get shot at."

But why? What was the point?

Then an unsettling fear filled Sara's mind. She eased away from Owen enough to reach the phone he'd given her. She pulled it out and dialed Anne.

The phone rang and rang. Anne didn't answer.

Panic filled her mind. Had something happened to Anne?

Was Juniper all right?

"Anne's not answering!" Sara said.

A third shot rang out, shaking the pine branches above them.

"Come on!" Owen said. "We've got to go."

"But what about Jess and Travis?" Sara asked.

"They'll be all right," Owen said.

She prayed it would be so.

Keeping low, they crawled single file until the trees thickened around them. Then Owen got to his feet, took Sara's hand and helped her up, and together they ran side by side down the hill toward his truck. They leaped in and Owen drove. The truck raced down the hill so quickly she could feel the tires skidding over the ice.

Prayers poured from Sara's lips for Anne, Travis, Jess and Derek. And for her little baby girl. Juniper had to be okay. She had to see her again.

A small blue car whizzed past them as they neared the Tatlows' house, driving so recklessly Owen had to swerve to miss it. A second later, they reached the house and leaped from the truck. The front door lay open in front of them. Anne was down on the floor in the entryway. Duct tape covered her mouth and bound her wrists.

Owen and Sara dropped to the floor beside her. Sara eased the tape off her mouth as Owen pulled out a pocketknife and cut her wrists free.

"Anne!" Sara said. "Are you okay? What happened?"

Tears filled the doctor's eyes.

"I'm sorry," Anne sobbed. "She took Juniper."

EIGHT

Sara glanced at Owen, and it was as if she could see his heart shatter in his chest. Their precious little daughter was gone? Juniper had been snatched away in the night by an unknown enemy because of something Sara had once done?

"It was that Delia woman," Anne said. "She lured me to open the door by pretending to be injured. I was so stupid. I'm sorry."

"Are you hurt?" Sara asked. She was still crouched down on the floor beside Anne. But Anne practically pushed her aside to get up.

"I'm fine," Anne said. "Don't worry about me. Please, you can still catch her. She just left. She was driving a blue car. Go! Go save your baby girl."

Owen leaped up and reached to grab Sara's hand, but she was already on her feet. He turned for the door, but Sara ran for the rack beside it and grabbed the chest-wrap carrier and Juniper's diaper bag.

"For when we find her," she said and felt her chin rise. "We are going to find her."

Fresh confidence filled his brokenhearted gaze. Anne grabbed her phone, and Sara saw she was dialing Jess.

Owen and Sara ran for the truck and hopped in. Owen peeled out and sped down the narrow rural highway in the direction they'd seen the blue car go. Desperately, her eyes searched the road ahead, praying with every breath that they'd see the headlights of the kidnapper's car, that they would find their baby and she would be all right. For a long moment, nothing but darkness lay ahead. Snow began to fall, and fear threatened to overwhelm her. Then she saw two tiny specks of light ahead of them in the distance, and she heard Owen say a prayer of thanks mingled with what sounded like a sob. He sped faster, and then they could see it was a small blue car just like the one they'd passed leaving the Tatlow farmhouse. Owen eased off the gas and held back. The car turned off the road and onto a narrow path between the trees.

Sara nearly cried out in shock and dismay when Owen drove right past it. The headlights disappeared behind them. What was he thinking? Everything inside her wanted to grab his hand—or even grab the steering wheel itself—and force him to turn the truck around. Instead, she gritted her teeth and forced herself to trust him. Seconds ticked past. She heard Owen count slowly backward from ten under his breath. Then he cut the lights, darkness enveloped them and only then did Owen turn the truck around and start driving slowly back toward where he saw the blue car turn.

Except now they couldn't see where the car had gone. The vehicle's headlights had disappeared. They inched along the highway, searching in vain for any sight of light. Neither of them spoke. She was beginning to despair when suddenly through the trees she saw a small rectangular window of light. There was some kind of cabin buried deep in the woods, and someone was inside it. She held her breath and prayed silently as Owen turned down a narrow path and drove toward it.

Then they saw the small blue car, sitting in front of a little cabin not much bigger than a shack.

Thank You, God.

Owen met her eyes.

"I'm going to park my truck across the drive so they can't escape," he said. "I'm guessing there's no point asking you to stay behind and wait in the truck?"

"I'm definitely coming with you," she said. Sara pulled out the phone and dialed both Jess and Travis in turn to let them know where they were and what was happening. Neither answered. She glanced at Owen. "Should we be worried they're not answering?"

"Maybe," he said.

They got out of the truck and started through the trees toward the cabin. She could hear the sound of her baby fussing.

Juniper!

She was there. She didn't sound hurt, but she was tired, confused and ready for bed.

She wanted her mommy and daddy.

"We're coming," Sara whispered.

They neared the house. What once might've been a small one-floor home was falling apart at the seams. Faded signs out front said it was for sale, and what she guessed were eviction notices were plastered on the door. But for some reason, the electricity was on inside the house. Faint light shone out the front window, with an even paler glimmer coming through what seemed to be a back door around the side.

Then she heard Delia's voice.

"Look, I went and got the kid for you!" Delia shouted. "I took it where you told me to take it. That makes us more than even. Now hurry up and get someone here! I'm not going to hang around here and play babysitter all night. I've done enough. My debt is paid."

Sara looked through the window. The main room lay empty except for their tiny daughter, who was fussing in her car seat, and Delia, who paced back and forth while she yelled into her phone.

Sara's eyes fixed on her small child. She prayed silently for God's help. Then Sara felt Owen's hand brush her arm. She reached for it, and his fingers closed over hers.

She took a deep breath, closed her eyes and let her mind focus. Then she felt an odd peace, both strange and yet familiar, move through her mind.

"We have to be smart," she said. "Normally, I'd say our best option would be for one of us to walk up to the front door and calmly try to negotiate with her, as a diversion, while the other one goes round the back and gets Juniper to safety. Only in this case, I'm not so sure it'll work."

She had no idea why she'd said "normally." But somehow she also knew she was right.

"And how do you know all this?" Owen asked.

"No idea," Sara said. "I just do."

Owen took a deep breath. "Okay. Let's say I trust you on that for now. What's your problem with that plan?"

"The problem," Sara said, "is that we know from her criminal history that she's volatile and unpredictable. Right now, she's agitated and angry, and the fact it's the middle of the night will make her even more erratic. She feels pushed into a corner, and I'm afraid if we try to go in there and negotiate with her, she'll dig her heels in and escalate this whole thing."

And put their daughter in even more danger.

"What if we had a gun?" Owen asked, "I'm not saying we do anything to risk her life, but we could injure her, disarm her and save Juniper."

She blinked. Did Owen have a weapon in his vehicle that he hadn't told her about?

"It would be incredibly hard to get a clean shot with her moving around like that, and firing a gun into the room with our baby in it is incredibly risky," she said. "It could ricochet."

Owen didn't respond for a long moment, and she suspected he was praying. Delia's yelling grew louder. Juniper's fussing began to crescendo to a full-on protest wail.

"So what do we do?" Owen asked.

"Honestly," Sara said, "and I can't believe I'm saying this, but my gut is saying that when you're dealing with someone this volatile, the best strategy is to overwhelm them with the unexpected." Though how she knew that strategy—and who'd taught it to her—she didn't know. "Something inside me wants to suggest we get in the truck and crash it right through the wall. Problem with that is—"

"Our baby's in there," Owen finished her thought.

"Exactly."

"All right," Owen said. "I have something in the truck that fits the bill, but I feel kind of ridiculous even saying it. Do you know what a tactical rescue light is?"

She shrugged. "Maybe."

"It's a gigantic flashlight," he said. "You could club somebody over the head with it if you had to. But it has all these settings with bright flashing lights and siren noises. It's really obnoxious. But if you're caught in a snowstorm and rescue teams are looking for you, it can save your life."

"Will it kill someone?" she asked.

"No, it'll temporarily blind them, disorient them and mess with their hearing though," he said. "Obviously we'd have to be very careful to protect Juniper and ourselves from the effects. But, most importantly, it'll create the kind of chaotic distraction you're talking about."

She felt a determined smile cross her lips. It wasn't a perfect plan, but he was listening to her and taking her seriously. She held his gaze for a long moment, wanting to say something she didn't even know how to put into words. What was more, she could see the same wordless thing echoed in his eyes.

"Fine!" Delia snapped into her phone. "Then hurry up! You better be here soon."

Delia ended the call but kept swearing and muttering angrily under her breath like a bubbling pot ready to boil over. They couldn't leave her alone with their baby a moment longer. Sara and Owen turned and ran for the truck. He opened the back storage compartment, pulled out the light and handed it to her. It was about five inches wide, a foot long and as heavy as a pumpkin, with a thick strap.

"You make the diversion, I take her down and then you go for our child?" he asked.

She nodded.

"I don't want Juniper to get hurt by either the sound

or the lights," she said. "So, I'll stay outside the building and be careful not to let the levels get too high. You should also probably throw a blanket over Juniper to shield her."

"I will," he said. "But this still leaves you at risk of being disoriented."

"I know," she said, "but I'll be smart. I won't look right at the light and I'll find something to plug my ears with so the noise won't be too loud."

He showed her the dimmer and switches. Then he gave her a one-armed hug, his lips brushing furtively over her cheek, before he disappeared swiftly through the trees. She pulled some cotton balls from the diaper bag, plugged her ears with it and the sounds of the world around her became muffled.

Sara walked up to the front door and prayed with every step.

Father God, please give us the strength, courage and wisdom we need to save our daughter's life.

She stopped about eight feet in front of the door, held the flashlight in front of her and switched the siren button all the way on. A shrill and piercing sound filled the air, whooping over and over again. Delia threw the door open and ran out. She aimed a small handgun at Sara's face.

"What are you doing? Turn that off now or I'll shoot you!" Delia shouted. Her eyes narrowed when she suddenly realized who was holding the siren. "You? You've absolutely ruined my life! I was doing just fine until you had to go and steal something, and somebody decided to make that my problem! Now tell me where those files are or I'm going to kill you and your kid!"

Sara gritted her teeth, shut her eyes and flicked another switch. Even with her eyes closed, she could see the blinding strobe light beam beating red against her eyelids.

Delia swore. Her gun fired.

Then she heard Owen's pounding footsteps as he charged from the darkness and the sound of Delia screaming and of her body hitting the porch.

"Sara!" Owen shouted. "She's down. Turn off the light and get Juniper!"

She switched the strobe light off and ran through the door for her child, past where Owen was on the ground wrestling Delia's hands behind her back. As promised, he'd draped a thick blanket over the car seat to shield Juniper from the noise and lights. Sara scooped Juniper up, still in her car seat, and pulled the blanket down far enough to see her face, and brushed a kiss over the top of her head.

"It's okay," she said. She could feel the tears of relief course down her cheeks. "Mommy's here. Mommy's got you."

She clutched Juniper's car seat to her chest, ran for the truck, threw the back door open and climbed inside. She buckled the car seat into the vehicle and then leaned past it to slam and lock the door. Then she looked through the windshield for Owen. She couldn't leave without him. But already he was pelting toward her. He leaped in the front seat, slammed the door and tossed what looked like Delia's gun in his glove compartment. Owen's eyes met hers in the rearview mirror.

"You okay?" he asked.

"We're good," Sara said and fished the cotton from her ears. "Drive."

He gunned the engine. The truck lurched forward a few feet, then Owen turned the steering wheel hard. The truck spun around, and they flew back down the narrow drive. Beside her in the back seat, Juniper began to calm, her cries dying down, from a combination of being somewhere warm, hearing her parents' voices and feeling the vehicle rumble beneath her. Sara reached into the diaper bag, pulled out Juniper's pacifier and offered it to her. The tiny girl grabbed it and shoved it into her mouth.

"What happened to Delia?" she asked.

"I tied her up and took her phone," Owen said, "I'll call Jess and she'll either arrest Delia herself or send a cop she trusts."

But no sooner had Owen said the words than they saw a large vehicle race up the highway behind them at what had to be twice the legal speed. It turned down the narrow path leading to the cabin where they'd left Delia.

"I'm guessing that's either whoever Delia was talking to or somebody sent by them," Sara said.

"We have to make sure they don't follow us," Owen said. "We'll get somewhere safe, and then we'll call Jess and Travis and brief them. And then we'll figure out our next move."

"Sounds good," she said.

Then she realized she hadn't heard from either of them since they'd escaped the gunfire in the graveyard. Sara hoped Travis, Jess and Derek were all right and that they'd gotten Derek to a hospital.

They drove through the darkness, down small country roads and through the trees, on paths so narrow she could barely see them. Long moments ticked past. Juniper's eyes closed, and the baby fell back into a peaceful sleep.

Then Owen brought the truck to a stop. Silence surrounded them. A long and shimmering lake lay in front of them, shining like a million diamonds in the darkness.

"I think we're alone," he said.

Sara unbuckled her seat belt and climbed in between the seats to get to the front passenger seat beside Owen. He unbuckled his seat belt too. Wordlessly, his eyes met hers. Something tugged hard inside her beating chest, like this invisible thread pulling her heart to his.

Suddenly, she reached for him. Her fingers slid along the edges of his jacket, then she clutched it tightly and pulled him toward her.

Their lips met.

His hands cupped her face and buried themselves in her hair. They kissed for one long moment, as relief, joy, fear and more feelings she couldn't even put into words crashed over her like a wave.

Then they pulled apart and stared at each other again. She watched as his mouth opened but no words came out.

She pulled the phone from her pocket. There was a voice mail from Jess. She put the phone on speaker and then held it up between them so Owen could hear it too.

"Sara! Owen!" Jess's voice was a desperate and panicked whisper. "Don't go back to the farmhouse. Police have raided it and found drugs someone planted in our house. Travis has been arrested. Anne and I have been brought in for questioning. Thankfully, Derek was unconscious but still alive when he was taken to the hospital. But the person who shot at us got away. Now our house is shut down as a crime scene. It's not safe to go back there. It's not safe to call or text us. I'm so sorry. You need to run. You are on your own!"

For a long moment, Owen sat there in stunned silence in the driver's seat of his truck, with Sara sitting equally quietly beside him and Juniper dozing in the back seat.

"Can you play it again?" he asked when he finally found his voice.

Sara played it again, and this time hearing Jess's words hit him even harder than before. Travis had been arrested on spurious drug charges, Jess and Anne were still being held without charges, their home was a crime scene...

His friends were in serious trouble, all because of him.

Wordlessly, he put his seat belt back on, waited until Sara buckled hers too and then backed up the truck and started driving. He drove without talking or thinking, or even knowing where he was going. Fear stabbed his chest at each new pair of headlights that appeared on the road, but as vehicle after vehicle passed without incident, he felt his pounding heart calm enough that he was able to think. He glanced at Sara. She was turning the phone over and over in her hands.

"How well do you know their hacker friend, Seth?" she asked.

"Not well," Owen admitted. "But Travis and Jess trust him with their lives. And with their kids' lives too."

"I have a good feeling about him also," she admitted. "I don't know why, but when I was talking to him, I had a gut feeling he was a good one."

"Me too," Owen said.

She dialed Seth, and the sound of the ringing phone filled the car.

"Hello?" Seth answered. He sounded no more awake or asleep than he had on the video chat hours before.

"Sorry to call in the middle of the night," she said. "It's Sara and Owen. Something bad happened."

She filled him in quickly on the empty grave, the gunfire at the grave site, Juniper's kidnapping, the drugs planted in the Tatlows' home, Jess and Anne being taken in for questioning, and Travis's arrest over the planted drugs.

Seth muttered a series of nonsensical syllables under his breath, like he was fighting the urge to swear and winning the battle. Then she heard him whisper a three-word prayer: "Help us, God.

"Okay," Seth said after taking a long breath. "Okay, okay, I've got a lot of people I've got to call and wake up right now. But don't worry, I've got this. Knowing Travis's security system, I won't be surprised if there's plenty of security-footage evidence of his innocence. It's just a matter of gaining access to it. Because Travis and Jess aren't going to turn it over to police without a warrant and will need to let someone they trust in on how to access it. Also, I've been doing a lot of digging into Sara's career in military intelligence and other stuff too. As agreed, I've only used legal means. No promises, but hopefully I'll have some solid stuff for you by the morning."

Owen had no idea what kind of "other stuff" Seth

was talking about. But beside him on the seat, Sara's entire body stiffened and her face paled. Now what was that about?

"You okay?" Owen whispered to her.

She nodded unconvincingly.

"Is there anything you guys need right now that I can help you with?" Seth asked.

"We have Delia's cellphone," Sara said.

"Okay, I'll arrange to pick it up from you and hack into it," Seth said. "There might be answers in there that'll blow this whole thing wide open."

"Hopefully," Owen said. "We need somewhere safe to go,"

Everything he owned was in Kilpatrick. His entire life was there.

"Okay," Seth said again. "I know people who can help with that. But it'll take a few hours. Maybe even a day or two."

"Right now, I want to go back to the Amish community where I was living," Sara said.

What? No, that wouldn't be safe.

"There's actually a really good unofficial witness-protection network within the Amish community in the United States," Seth suggested. "Nothing official through law enforcement. All volunteers."

No, that was an even worse idea. Owen couldn't give up everything to disappear into a new life and identity with the Amish. Could he?

"Something someone on the video chat said stuck with me," Sara interjected. "She said the files could've been on a small memory card that could've been sewn into the hem of my clothes or something. I want to go back to the Zooks' farmhouse and see if I can find what I was wearing when Petrus and Hadassah rescued me. Delia seems absolutely convinced that I have some kind of files that really bad people want. I don't know if there will be anything left after the fire. But if we can find those files and figure out what they are, we might be able to end all this."

There was a long pause, as if Seth was debating this idea just as hard as Owen was.

"I don't like it," Owen said, "but it's a really smart idea."

"Agreed," Seth said.

Owen wished there was a way he could go by himself to keep Sara out of danger. But it made sense for her to do it. And he felt they'd all be safer if the three of them stuck together.

"We need to go in undercover," Sara said, "the best we can. Whoever's behind this might have someone on the lookout for the truck. So is there any way you can get us a horse and buggy?"

Seth sputtered a cross between a cough and a laugh. Sara smiled slightly.

"Can't say I've ever tried to source an Amish horse and buggy in the middle of the night before," he said. "But I'm always up for a challenge. I'll make sure to have a buggy and also a pack of supplies waiting for you at an Amish market off the grid, and someone who'll take your truck off you and keep it safe."

"Thank you." Owen let out a long breath. "How will we know who this person is?"

"I'll stick a bow on it," Seth said and laughed. Then his tone turned serious. "Any friends of Travis and Jess are friends of mine. We've gotten each other out of more than a few life-or-death situations."

"And when we get out of this mess," Sara said, "if there's any way we can help you or anyone else in the future, don't hesitate to give me a call."

"Ditto for me," Owen said.

"Will do," Seth said. "But for now, what are you going to do if you don't find the files right away and this thing drags on? You want me to put out feelers to my friends in the States to see if we can find you a long-term place to stay?"

Owen felt his jaw clench. "Hopefully it won't come to that," he said.

They ended the call, and silence filled the truck again. Then he heard the soft and gentle sound of Sara praying underneath her breath, and he joined in prayer alongside her. After a while, her voice quieted, and when he glanced her way, he saw she'd tucked her scarf into the crook of her neck and was leaning her head against the window. But even though her eyes eventually closed, he suspected she never actually fell asleep. After an hour, she opened her eyes again and offered to take a turn driving. But he didn't have much more success sleeping than she did.

The snow had stopped falling and the sun was rising slowly in warm orange and golden hues over the horizon when they finally reached the Amish market.

The remote market sat all alone on a rural highway surrounded by fields on all sides. The building was the size of a warehouse and looked more like a series of interconnected barns with one huge barn in the middle. Dawn was still breaking, and yet there were already over a dozen buggies and a smattering of trucks and cars scattered around the huge lot. They pulled over to the far side, where a dark-haired young man who was clad in blue jeans and a jacket, and looked no more than eighteen, stood beside a beautiful dappled gray horse, harnessed to a small black buggy, with a red bow around its neck. He and Sara gathered their things, got out of the truck and walked over to him, with Juniper's car seat in one of Owen's hands and her diaper bag slung over his shoulder.

"You're Seth's friends?" the kid asked.

"Yup," Owen said.

"I put a few things in a bag in the back for you," the kid said. "Some food, a burner phone in case yours is being tracked and a couple of changes of clothes. He told me to take your phone if you're willing to part with it and also said you might not be able to get your hands on cash for a while, so there's five hundred in an envelope underneath it. Call Seth when you're ready to get your truck and phone back, and someone will tell you where to meet up."

"Thank you," Owen said.

"So, the burner phone doesn't have a tracker?" Sara asked.

"It's untraceable by any outside means, if that's what you mean," the boy said. "Nobody can trace the signal. But Seth put a tiny physical tracking device inside the case so he can find you in an emergency." He shrugged. "I said you might throw it out if I told you. But he said it was your choice whether to keep it on you or not. And that you were suspicious enough of everything that you'd find it anyway."

Owen chuckled under his breath. He noticed that the kid hadn't introduced himself or offered any personal information, and remembered the promise he himself had made to help others in need. He found himself praying that one day, when all this was done, he'd have the opportunity to be the one helping out someone else in trouble. Owen handed over his cell phone, Delia's phone and the keys to his truck.

Sara turned to Owen.

"When you disarmed Delia, you put the gun in the glove compartment, right?" she asked. "Is it still there? We're not taking it into the Amish community."

"Yes, it's still in the truck," he said truthfully.

But the gun he'd worn to the graveyard was still hidden in his ankle holster inside his pant leg. He hadn't told her he had it yet, and the weight of that seemed to grow heavier with every step.

Sara turned to the boy. "Tell Seth about the gun. I'm sure he'll know what to do with it."

The young man nodded again. They watched as he got into the truck and left.

"I just hope my truck fares better than my snowmobile did," Owen said.

He grinned weakly. But Sara's eyes were serious as she searched his face.

"You're good with people," she said, and he felt an odd heat rise to the back of his neck. "Come on, let's get some supplies."

They put the car seat and diaper bag in the buggy, then Sara swaddled Juniper to her chest with a long piece of cloth. Together they crossed the parking lot to the market. The warm and welcoming scent of fresh baking filled his senses as he stepped inside. They started off surrounded on all sides by a lush and colorful array of fruits, vegetables, flowers, nuts and seeds in bins and baskets. From there they moved into the large bakery section, where the delicious smells had been coming from. Along with rolls and loaves of bread of all kinds, shapes and sizes, there were also meat and fruit pies and fresh egg sandwiches. Owen's stomach rumbled. The bakery gave way to shelves of canned and jarred goods.

Sara filled a basket full of food, and then they walked up a narrow flight of stairs to the second floor. There he found books and Bibles in both English and German, as well as maps for Pennsylvania Dutch Country. They moved past them into aisles and aisles of clothes. Sara selected two dresses, one plain black and another in soft blue, along with bonnets, aprons and pins for her hair. In the next aisle over, she found matching clothes for Juniper. Then she showed him the aisles of men's clothes. The shirts and pants were black and fastened with hooks and eyes instead of buttons. But he was impressed by the quality of the fabric and craftsmanship, and the work boots were the sturdiest he'd ever seen. Sara helped him select clothes and a hat, then she got him a straight razor to shave with.

"Amish men don't have moustaches," she explained, "so you'll have to shave it off to go undercover. Married men have beards, but single men do not."

She paused. He'd left his own wedding ring in a drawer in his bedroom back in his apartment above the hardware store. After they'd separated, and then after he thought she'd died, he'd worn it some days and not others, depending on how he felt. But it was a small token that the rest of the world couldn't see if he slid his hand in his pocket.

This would literally be writing his relationship status on his face.

"It's up to you what you decide to do," Sara added. "But as a man of marrying age traveling with a woman and child, you'll attract less attention if you keep your beard."

He nodded. "Okay, sounds good."

They made their purchases, and then she took Juniper into the women's change room. He went into the men's room, ran hot water in the sink and shaved his moustache off. After staring at his reflection for a long moment, he decided to keep the beard. Then he got changed, surprised at how comfortable everything was. Once again, he fastened the holster around his ankle and hid it under the leg of his pants. His hand touched the door handle, but before pushing the door open, he paused and prayed.

Lord, this thing I'm embarking on is so different from everything I've ever known. I don't know if trying to find these files and some memory card in Sara's clothes is just a wild-goose chase. Or what will happen if we don't find it. For months I was sure I felt You calling me to care for Kilpatrick and build up the town. Now I've literally fled my home with nothing but the clothes on my back. Be my guide and fill me with Your wisdom and Your strength.

Then he opened the door and stepped out. He found Sara and Juniper waiting for him outside by the horse and buggy, both dressed in simple dark dresses and white bonnets. Sara turned to face him. Juniper waved her arms and giggled, and Sara's eyes met his.

His breath caught in his throat.

She was stunning. Something about the simplicity of the clothing made her natural beauty shine through. He reached up and self-consciously ran his hand over his beard, feeling the odd contrast of his soft upper lip against his thumb, and for a moment he didn't know what to say.

"Do I look okay?" he asked.

She nodded. "You look wonderful."

Bright winter sunlight illuminated her features, but it was nothing compared to the dazzling light that seemed to shine through her eyes.

They walked over to one of the picnic tables that were dotted around the front of the market, fed Juniper breakfast and ate something quickly themselves. The parking lot was beginning to fill up now as both those dressed in *plain* garb and *Englischer* clothes mingled together, talking and sharing smiles over the fresh baked goods and coffee. They had to get going.

"You okay to take the reins?" she asked.

"Absolutely," he said. He offered Sara his hand and helped her and Juniper up into the buggy. Then he walked around to the other side, ran his hand down the horse's neck and greeted him softly. Owen climbed up and flicked the reins, and the horse started trotting. Sara dug in the bag for a warm blanket. She draped it over both of them then took Juniper out of her chest harness and let their daughter bounce on her lap. He felt Sara's leg brush against his under the blanket.

"I don't think I ever told you all that much about my

life growing up in Kilpatrick," he said. "Back when we met, I was so focused on trying to get my future sorted out I didn't fully appreciate what was special about my past. When I was a kid, a friend of my family owned horses, and they were a huge part of the winter fair. We'd set up this little area with bales of hay and a wood corral, where kids could go on pony rides around in a circle. There'd be sleigh rides going up and down the street with bells jingling and the whole bit."

He felt a wide smile crinkle his face.

"That was actually my first real job," he said. "I started leading the pony rides when I was about twelve, and then when I was fifteen, I got to drive the sleigh. I don't know why I never told you about that. Maybe it was because we lived in the big capital city of Ottawa, and my small-town traditions seemed so small. But I really loved it. I don't know why, but I just seem to have a way with horses. They like me, and I know how to communicate with them."

"People like you too, Mayor," Sara said.

Unexpected heat rose to his cheeks. He took a deep breath and let the cold air fill his lungs.

"The fair was very, very different back then," he added. "We didn't have ice displays or fireworks. We made our own hot chocolate and gingerbread instead of bringing in gourmet chefs. There were baking competitions, and people sold local jams and jellies."

"It sounds wonderful," she said.

"It was. You would've really loved it."

Then he frowned. "The fair got bigger, and the town got smaller," he added.

He stared out at the endless line of snow-covered fields for a long minute as he searched for an analogy.

"Imagine you've got an orchard, and one day you notice that while you have a lackluster crop, there's this one magic tree in the middle of the garden that grows apples of pure gold. So you stop watering and feeding your other plants and put everything you've got into the golden tree, until it's all you have. Then one day, you realize you've been putting so much fertilizer and water into that one tree, it barely grows more gold than it costs. But what can you do? You've let all your other plants die, and what do you do then?" He sighed. "I don't know if that analogy makes sense."

"It does." She reached over, took his hand and squeezed it for a long moment before letting go. The horse and buggy plodded on. It had been years since he'd ridden in a sleigh or buggy, and he hadn't realized how much he'd missed it. The sky stretched blue and endless above him. Cars whizzed past in a blur, scattered houses and farms came and went, and fields of white filled his view in every direction. An hour passed, and then a second.

Then he heard a deep and pain-filled gasp slip from Sara's lips, making his own heart stop in response.

"What's wrong?"

"There!" She pointed to the trees. "That's where the farm was!"

He couldn't even see where she was pointing at first. He pulled down a narrow drive and stopped.

There, against the pure white snow, a wide patch of charred black wood lay like a wound. Sara pressed Juniper into his hands before tumbling from the buggy and running for the scorched earth. She fell to her knees in the snow and buried her hands in the ash. He tucked Juniper into the crook of his arm and climbed down from the buggy, feeling the small balloon of hope that he hadn't even realized had been floating inside him pop as he surveyed the damage. Even if there had been a memory card hidden inside Sara's clothes, there was no way it would've survived the blaze. Wordlessly, he walked over and laid a hand on her shoulder.

"This used to be the front entrance," she said. Then she pointed with soot-covered fingers over to her right, where he could barely see the remains of a kitchen pot sticking out among the jagged edges of broken boards.

"That was the kitchen. And I think over there are the remains of the staircase. That patch of burned boards over there used to be the barn and the chicken coops. The horses were gone when I escaped the house. I hope they're okay."

She looked up at him. Tears streaked her cheeks.

"It's all gone," she said. "There's no hope of finding anything in these ashes. It's all been destroyed, and there's nothing left."

A branch cracked. Owen turned sharply to see something rustle in the trees.

They weren't alone.

NINE

Owen searched the brush with his eyes and spotted a young boy of about ten or eleven in Amish clothing.

"Hey!" Owen yelled.

The boy's eyes widened. He turned and took off running over the fields.

"Hey!" Owen yelled again. He straightened up and was about to hand Juniper to Sara and dash after him when Sara grabbed his hand.

"It's okay," she said. "I think he's gone to get help."

"How can you possibly know that?" he asked.

"I can't," she said. She cleaned her hands in the snow and stood slowly. "But I have to have faith."

A few moments later, a horse-drawn sleigh appeared through the trees, headed by an Amish man with a gray beard and salt-and-pepper hair. A cry of joy slipped her lips.

"Dr. Amos!" Sara called. She ran toward him across the snow as he pulled the sleigh to a stop. "Owen, this is Petrus Zook's brother, the doctor he sent for to care for me."

At a closer glance, the doctor looked younger than Owen had first thought, and he guessed he was in his fifties. His keen eyes peered at Owen with a curiosity bordering on suspicion. But as he looked past Owen to Sara, palpable relief and joy crossed the man's features. Then he said something in a language Owen couldn't understand, but which Owen's heart could tell were prayers of thanksgiving.

"Sara!" he said. He leaped down from the sleigh. "I am so thankful to see you."

She walked over to him, and they exchanged warm greetings.

"Was anyone hurt in the fire?" she asked. "Are the animals okay?"

"Thankfully, we managed to stop it from spreading," he said. "We found the horses wandering, and they are now in our barn. My children were able to rescue most of the chickens."

Sara thanked God silently. Then she turned to Owen and introduced them.

"This is the doctor I told you about who took such good care of me," she said. "Dr. Amos, this is Owen."

"Ah, he is your *mann*," the doctor said. Then he turned to Owen. "That means *husband*."

Owen blinked. "How could you tell I'm not Amish?" he asked.

"Something about your body language," Amos said. The man smiled gently. "You don't stand like a man who's heart has known peace." Then he glanced at Juniper, who was still tucked in the crook of Owen's arm, and his eyes misted slightly. "And who is this?"

"My daughter," Sara said. "Juniper."

"She's lovely," he said.

Something about the way the man spoke made Owen

think he was used to talking to non-Amish people. Although Owen still didn't understand how he could be both a doctor and Amish, he felt incredibly thankful to him for helping save Sara's life. While the doctor's smile was professional, his brows knit and an almost-analytical look filled his eyes, which made Owen feel like he was being scrutinized. Owen suddenly realized the doctor had suspected that he might've been the one behind Sara's injury.

Maybe she realized it too, because she touched his arm protectively.

"Owen had been tricked into thinking I was dead," Sara said. "He was very surprised to discover I was still alive."

"Really?" Amos's eyebrows rose.

Should Sara be telling him this, trusting him with this information? Owen reached for her hand and squeezed it in a silent warning. She squeezed it back, and somehow Owen knew she was telling him to trust her.

The doctor nodded. The look of concern in his eyes deepened.

"Two criminals broke into the farmhouse," she continued. "They were looking for something they thought I stole. So I came back, hoping to look at the clothes I was wearing when Petrus found me, in case I'd sewn something into the seams or forgotten about something I had in my pockets. But they were lost in the fire."

"I have your clothes at my home," Dr. Amos said. "They were tattered and torn, but I kept them in case you ever asked to see them."

Hope rose in Owen's chest, and he saw it mirrored in Sara's eyes.

"Brain injuries are tricky," the doctor continued. "You had clearly experienced trauma, and I wanted to be cautious and wait until you were ready." Owen remembered that Anne had said something similar about not telling Sara too much information too quickly. "Also, I expect my brother, Petrus, and Hadassah to call our community phone booth tomorrow to let us know they've arrived safely. You can stay as our guests tonight and talk to them tomorrow. They might have more information."

It wasn't the worst idea, and it was a generous offer, Owen thought. After all, Seth hadn't called back with any leads on a safe house. They needed a place to rest and sleep, and if they didn't find what they were looking for in Sara's clothes, talking to the couple who'd rescued her might help.

"That is very kind of you," Owen said. "But we don't know who the criminals after us are, and they might track us here. I don't want to bring danger to your door."

The doctor's chin rose.

"When my brother and his wife chose to take you in, they knew they might be risking their lives," he said to Sara. "And I knew the same when I came to help treat your wounds. We have faith that if we are following God's will, God will protect us. Now come. You can stay the night in the *grossdaadi haus* and celebrate Old Christmas with us tomorrow."

He turned and went back to his sleigh and guided his horses down the road. Owen and Sara followed in the buggy.

"What did he mean by that?" Owen asked.

"*Grossdaadi* means grandfather," Sara said. "A *gross-*

daadi house is a small home behind the main house, for an elderly relative. They invited me to stay with them when Petrus and Hadassah left, as a single woman shouldn't be living alone. But I wanted to stay and take care of the farm."

"Okay, and what did he mean by Old Christmas?" he asked. It was January. Christmas was almost two weeks ago and already felt like a distant memory.

"The Amish celebrate Christmas on January 6," she said. "It's much simpler than English Christmas and focused on community. There will be a big family meal and a children's concert with music and readings." A smile crossed her lips as she thought of it. Then as he watched, worry filled her eyes. "I hope we made the right decision coming here and are able to find what we're looking for to put this behind us."

He hoped so too. But then what would happen to this fragile peace they'd found between them?

The farmhouse of the doctor's family was large and simple, set in a beautiful backdrop of snow-covered trees. The same small boy they'd seen earlier was waiting for them outside. Amos introduced him as his eldest grandson, Jonathan. As Jonathan went to care for the horses, they stepped inside the farmhouse, where they were greeted by a smiling gray-haired woman, whom Amos introduced as his wife, Ruth. She was holding a small child on her hip, their youngest grandchild, Miriam. Ruth greeted Sara warmly, and the two women embraced.

Soon the rest of the family joined them, excited to see Sara again and happy to know she was safe. As Sara introduced Owen to Amos's five children and the other grandchild, Amos pulled his wife aside for a quiet word. When they returned, Amos was carrying a covered basket. He led Sara and Owen through the kitchen, out a side door and along a narrow snow-covered path to a much smaller house set in the trees behind the large house.

The *grossdaadi* house was a tiny home with just two main rooms—a kitchen and living area in the front, and a small bedroom in the back. A warm blanket lay over the back of the one rocking chair and another over the end of the bed. A fire crackled from the wood-burning stove, and an oil lamp hung on a hook above their heads, softly illuminating the room. A larger basket of food and baby supplies sat on the simple wooden table. Amos set his small basket beside it and invited them to join the family in the main house whenever they were ready. Then he left them alone.

Owen spread a blanket down on the floor, helped Juniper out of her winter clothes and set her on the blanket. She gurgled happily and immediately got to work trying to crawl. Sara opened the smaller basket, looked inside and gasped. He watched as she started to pull out the clothes she'd been found in six months earlier.

"Are you okay?" he asked.

She shook her head and for a long moment didn't speak as she laid a pair of jeans, a T-shirt, sweatshirt and sneakers side by side on the counter. Pain turned in his chest. They were ripped and torn and so caked in brown streaks of what he guessed was a combination of dirt and blood it was virtually impossible to tell what color they'd originally been. He stepped behind her and slid a protective arm around the small of her back. She leaned into him as her hands slowly ran over the clothes. Something tightened in his throat. He'd known she'd survived being shot and had taken months to recover. But until this moment, he'd never realized just how close she'd come to death.

He closed his eyes and prayed, thanking God for saving her life and asking Him to bring the criminals responsible to justice and end this nightmare forever.

"There's nothing here either," she said. He opened his eyes and stepped back as she turned to look at him. "I've checked every inch of the fabric. The clothes practically fell apart at the seams, and there's no memory stick. No files." He looked down at her hands. She was twisting a small square of soft white fabric between her fingers. She handed it to him. "It was in my inside pocket. That's why it's still clean. But there's nothing special about it."

He glanced at it, then turned to look at the clothes on the table. Slowly and meticulously, he went over each item too, pulling the seams apart with his fingers and feeling for any discrepancy or lump under the fabric. Finally, he had to agree she was right. There was nothing there.

"I don't get it," Sara said. "The people who came after me all seemed convinced I had these files on me. But I didn't. There's nothing here!"

He reached for her, wanting to wrap his arms around her and comfort her. But instead, she walked away, pulled out the cell phone and called Seth. Owen waited as she quickly told him where they were, that they'd found nothing so far and that they'd wait until tomorrow to talk to Petrus and Hadassah on the common phone. The entire call lasted less than a minute.

Then she hung up and turned to Owen.

"That was fast," he said.

"He doesn't think anyone's tracking our phone, but he wanted to be extra cautious," she said. "The good news is he's found no chatter implying we've been followed or traced here. The best news is that Derek is still alive in the hospital."

"And the bad news?"

"Anne and Jess still haven't been released. Police can detain you twenty-four hours without laying charges. Travis has been actually charged. Also, Seth is looking into finding us a safe house, but nothing's come through yet. He suggests we stay put for now. Hopefully when I get to talk to Petrus and Hadassah tomorrow, one of them will remember something helpful."

"So what do we do now?" he asked.

"I don't know," she said. "I guess we wait and pray."

They went to the farmhouse and rejoined the doctor's family. The rest of the day stretched out long and peaceful, like the quiet respite in the middle of a storm. And despite the fear in his heart, as the hours passed, Owen felt an odd peace begin to coexist inside him. He joined Amos's sons and grandsons in helping out with chores around the farm, Sara helped her friends in the kitchen and Juniper played on the floor with the other children. As night fell, the family joined around the table for a delicious meal of chicken, gravy, potatoes, vegetables and fresh bread. It was so clear that Sara had a close connection with this family and they'd embraced her as one of them.

As the sun began to set, Owen found himself standing alone on the front porch, watching as orange streaks painted the white-capped trees. He couldn't remember the last time he'd gone this long without his phone and wondered how many calls he'd missed from the residents of Kilpatrick.

If he was honest, Owen had probably never stopped to think through, let alone imagine, what his idea of a perfect day would be. If he had, it probably wouldn't have involved him wearing a straw hat or sporting an unfamiliar beard. But despite the strangeness of the outside trappings, he knew in his heart it wouldn't have been that different from how the day had unfolded. Yes, the underlying sense of fear and dread had been a constant presence in the pit of his stomach, and he'd seen it reflected in Sara's eyes as well. And yet, in other moments he'd also seen Sara happy, relaxed, comfortable and at peace in a way he never had before. He'd watched his baby giggle and squeal as she played with other kids. He'd been surrounded by good people who believed in having faith and taking care of one another. It was the closest thing he'd felt in a long time to how he remembered growing up in his hometown. And it stirred a deep longing inside him for something he didn't even know how to put into words.

He heard the door open and looked to see Amos coming out to join him. They nodded to each other and for a long moment stood side by side in silence, much as he had with Travis the previous morning.

"I've been speaking to some friends in the community," the doctor said, "and no one has seen any strangers around, or anyone asking about you or Sara. So far, it seems nobody has tracked you here."

Owen let out a breath he didn't know he'd been holding.

"We spoke to a hacker friend of ours, and he said the same," Owen replied. "That there hasn't been any chatter online about our location. But either way, we'll be leaving tomorrow after Sara manages to talk to Petrus and Hadassah on the phone." He paused and wondered if he had to explain to the Amish man what the internet and hackers were. "I'm sorry," Owen added, "but I'm confused—are you a real doctor?"

Amos chuckled and ran his hand over his beard. "Yes. I went to Canadian Mennonite University for my undergraduate. There is a much larger Mennonite community in Canada than Amish. Then I went to medical school in Winnipeg. Now, I spend a lot of my time as a doctor in the community, but also work in the hospital. There are a lot of people who've found a way to combine their *plain* way of life with work that involves technology. They may have electricity or computers at their workplace but rely on the traditional way of life at home."

"I didn't know people did that," Owen admitted.

Amos nodded. "Maybe it would help you to think of my faith as spiritual practices that are meant to bring me closer to God and my community. My path brings me peace."

The older man's words were still running through Owen's head as he walked through the snow to the *grossdaadi* house, where Sara was getting Juniper ready for bed. Did his own way of life bring him peace? When all this was over, what would peace even look like? For Travis, finding his place in the world had meant giving up his job as a detective, but for Jess it had meant keeping hers. He'd assumed Sara had loved her life in military intelligence, and yet he'd never seen her as happy as she was today.

As for himself, he felt like he'd spent years trying to put his hometown's family legacy in the rearview mirror only to end up discovering it was where he felt he belonged.

He opened the door to the cabin. Soft and warm light glowed from the lamp. Sara sat on the floor on the blanket with Juniper. She looked up as he came in, and for a long moment neither of them said anything. He sat down in the rocking chair, planted his heels into the floor and rested his elbows on his knees.

"I know you don't remember this," Owen said, "but when we met, I spent so much time complaining about the town where I grew up and acting like I thought I was too good for that life. I was like a fish flopping all around on the dock, protesting that I didn't like the water."

She chuckled softly at the analogy.

"I've been so hard on the residents of Kilpatrick for wanting to throw money at the winter fair," he added. "Like they're trying to throw stuff at the wall and see what sticks. But I started three different university programs I dropped out of."

He paused and ran his hand over the back of his neck. What was he trying to say?

"When we were together, I used to beat myself up for not being more successful or having more money. I wasn't happy with myself, and I projected all that onto you. I told myself that you didn't think I was good enough and that you wanted me to be different. I blamed you for how I felt about me. It wasn't until I lost you that I even tried to find peace within myself. How could I blame you for the fact I hadn't found happiness when I didn't even try?"

Sara didn't answer, and yet the way her beautiful blue eyes searched his face told him she'd heard every word. Silence fell between them again. He looked down at Juniper and watched as her happy babbling quieted and her nose wrinkled with the telltale sign that she'd need sleep soon. When he glanced back at Sara, something sad had washed over her gaze, and she wore the same distant look she'd had after she escaped Delia the first time.

"What are you thinking?" he asked.

"I'm thinking about the fact I still don't know who I am," she said. "As much as I loved spending time here today, my past is always going to find me. And what if it turns out I've done criminal things? What if I've hurt people? Or done things that are unforgivable?"

He dropped from the chair and knelt beside her on the floor, taking her hands in his.

Did she know something he didn't?

"Don't say that. I promise that whatever is hidden in your past and whatever you've done, God will forgive you, and we can move past it."

For a long moment her fingers lingered in his. Then she pulled away.

"You can't say that. Because maybe I've done some really bad things that will hurt you in ways you couldn't ever forgive me for. And that I'll never forgive myself for either."

* * *

They decided Sara would sleep in the bedroom with Juniper, Owen would take the front room and they'd stay fully clothed with their boots on, so that they'd be able to run at the first sign of trouble. When it was Sara's turn to sleep, she didn't expect she'd be able to nod off. Instead she lay there praying and listening to the sounds of the snow buffeting gently against the window, the fire crackling in the stove and the creak of Owen rocking back and forth in the chair.

Then suddenly she was dreaming—the same dream as usual, only sharper and clearer this time, as if someone had turned up the color and sound. She was terrified and running for her life. Fear and pain pounded through her. She could hear the same roar as before, only now it was a voice, loud and angry, calling her vile names and threatening to kill her, Juniper and everyone she loved unless she gave him back the files. She heard herself cry out in pain.

"Sara." Owen's voice was gentle and firm. "It's okay. You're only dreaming. You're in the *grossdaadi* house. I'm here. You're with me. I've got you. You're safe."

She felt the floorboards creak as he knelt down beside her and felt the touch of his strong hands as he tenderly brushed the hair back from her face. He was there beside her. She wasn't alone. She reached for his hand and clutched it tightly. His thumb ran over her fingers, and a deep peace flowed through her body. She fell back asleep.

She woke hours later, feeling more rested than she had in a long time, to the sound of Juniper crying out to greet the morning sun and Owen's snores coming from the living room. She gathered her baby into her arms, changed and dressed Juniper, and walked through the door to find Owen curled up on the blanket on the floor. Something warm swelled in her heart as she looked down at him. She reached for the ring she wore on the chain around her neck and rolled it under her fingertips.

Owen had turned out to be nothing like she'd imagined. He'd been much more stubborn, definitely uncertain and quick to disagree with her. He hadn't given her any of the answers to uncover what had happened to her, and had instead piled on even more questions. And yet, he'd also been kind and courageous, with a heart that was wide open to the people who needed him and a mind that was eager to learn. It was so clear how she'd once fallen in love with him and why it was so tragic that their love had fallen apart.

Owen's eyes fluttered open and a sheepish grin crossed his face. "You all right?"

"Yeah," she said. "Thank you for coming to help me when I got trapped in that nightmare."

"Anytime."

"It was terrifying," she went on. "This time there was a voice too. He was shouting at me and threatening to kill us."

"Hey, it's okay." Owen leaped to his feet and took her free hand in his. "I'm here now."

But how long would he be there? And how long would she let him be?

Then Owen wrapped one arm around her waist and pulled her closer to him, with their small child still nestled in one arm between them. He leaned forward. So did Sara, and she felt her forehead against his.

"I don't want to lose you again," she whispered.

"Maybe you don't have to." His voice was husky in his throat. She tilted her chin up toward him and felt his lips brush quickly and furtively over hers.

The loud and tinny sound of a phone ringing shattered the silence. They leaped apart, and for a moment both searched for the cell phone as the sound grew louder and louder until it seemed to press against the walls. Juniper began to cry, her wails mixing with the sound. Then finally Owen found it in the basket on the counter. There was a missed call from Seth and a text telling Sara to call him urgently.

Sara glanced at Owen and then out the window. Two of Amos's children were standing outside the kitchen door with confused looks on their faces. Sara waved at them and the children waved them toward the door, as if beckoning them in for breakfast.

"I think they heard it," Sara said. "It's pretty quiet around here and sound travels. Do you mind taking Juniper in for food while I call Seth? I won't be able to hear him over the sound of her crying."

And she was afraid that whatever he was going to tell her wasn't good news.

She waited and watched as Owen bundled Juniper up in a blanket and walked with her through the snow to the farmhouse then disappeared through the kitchen door. She steeled a breath and called Seth's number.

"Hello!" the hacker answered before the phone had even rung once.

"Hey, it's Sara. Sorry we missed your call."

"Is Owen with you?" he asked.

"No," she said. "He's in the main house with Juniper and the family that's sheltering us."

"Okay," Seth said. He seemed to be chewing over the word as if debating what to say next. "That might be good. I've got a bunch to unload, and you might need a moment alone to unpack it."

Yeah, she'd been afraid of that.

She sat down in the rocking chair and braced herself. "Hit me."

He started with the good news that Travis, Jess and Anne had all been released and Travis's charges were dropped after Bert called the station, told them he was their lawyer and threatened to bring the full might of the law against them if they didn't allow him access to his clients immediately.

"He's a crotchety geezer at times," Seth said about the man Sara remembered had made pointed remarks during the video call. "But he means well and is an excellent criminal lawyer."

"Thank You, God," Sara prayed.

"After that, it took mere moments for Travis to get him access to the home security footage," Seth added, "which of course proved that Travis was innocent and a cop planted the drugs."

"Let me guess—that cop's been arrested but isn't talking," Sara said. "Plus he has no known connection to any of the other criminals in this case."

"Right you are," Seth said. "So far nobody's turning on the big baddy who hired them. Derek's in a medically induced coma. But very much alive, and it's too early to start worrying he won't pull through and be able to tell us more about who told him to cremate the body, bury an empty coffin and then go rushing to the graveyard in the middle of the night to get shot."

She listened as he took a deep breath and blew it out hard.

"Also, I found out some interesting information about your history in military intelligence," Seth went on. "All through legal, confidential channels. Apparently you'd been in elite and specialized training for overseas assignment in covert intelligence operations."

She let out a long breath. "Like a real spy?"

"Like a very real spy, with combat training and the ability to take out bad guys in close quarters," Seth confirmed. "Apparently your skills with a gun are legendary."

"Which explains a lot," she said.

"But is about as helpful as telling a mermaid that she had once been a really fast runner?" Seth asked.

"You mean because that life is behind me, and I don't want to go back to it?" she asked. "True."

"Hey, I get it," Seth said. "Former criminal here. But you might be interested to know that you were apparently in line for a plum overseas assignment when you met Owen and turned it down to be with him. You turned down two more similar assignments after that. For what it's worth, people thought you really loved the guy, more than your career."

Okay, then why would Delia have told her she'd drawn up legal papers trying to keep him from having anything to do with her or Juniper?

"That all?" she asked.

"Not quite. Are you sitting down? Because Tess pulled

off the near impossible." He paused dramatically. "She found your old roommate, Casey Brown."

Relief poured over Sara like a flood, and she hadn't realized until that moment just how worried she'd been that Casey had been the woman buried in her place.

"So she's alive," Sara confirmed.

"Very much so," Seth said. "After she heard you were murdered, she decided to drop off the grid and go traveling the world. It made her reevaluate life."

"Did you tell her I'm alive?" Sara asked.

"No," Seth said. "I figured that information was still need to know. But she was very happy to talk to me all about the investigation into your murder. Turns out, she's convinced Owen murdered you."

"You're kidding!"

Sara's eyes ran to the indentation in the blankets where he'd been curled up asleep not thirty minutes earlier.

Seth sighed.

"The bad news is that all those legal documents that Delia told you about were true," he said. "You did ask the real Casey to draw all that up for you to force a review of Owen's finances, end his parental rights, and keep him away from you and Juniper. You didn't tell her why, and so when you died she told the police all of it. That's probably how whoever blackmailed Delia into kidnapping you and Juniper knew what to tell her. They have another mole within law enforcement."

Tears burned her eyes.

Why would I have ever contemplated doing something so cruel to Owen?

She and Seth ended the call soon afterward, with the

promise that she'd call him after she spoke to Petrus and Hadassah and they were ready to leave the Ontario Amish community. Then she hid the phone in her apron and joined the family in the farmhouse, where they were still in the middle of breakfast. While her eyes told her that the meal was warm and delicious, every bite tasted like sawdust in her mouth.

She pulled Owen aside after the meal and filled him in on the news about Travis being out of jail, Derek being in a coma and Casey still being alive. But she didn't tell him the rest. How could she?

He had saved her life, and she'd tried to destroy his.

She'd wait until the Old Christmas celebrations were over and she'd talked to Petrus and Hadassah, then she'd tell him the truth.

The family gathered in the living room to open some simple handmade gifts for the children. Then they all piled into sleighs and traveled into town for the children's Christmas concert in the meeting hall. The children took their places to sing songs and do readings. But as adorable as they were, Sara couldn't pull her gaze away from Owen's face. His eyes shone as he watched them perform. He sat forward on the wooden bench with his hands on his knees. In the months she'd spent recovering in this community, she'd never dared dream that one day Owen would join her here. Now he had. And as soon as the celebrations were over and they left town again, she'd be telling him a truth that would break his heart.

When the concert ended, Owen took Juniper from her and went to congratulate the children on their performance.

But Sara sat alone on the wooden bench, her heart too heavy for her feet to move.

Suddenly, a large man sat down beside her. She felt the bench shift under his weight.

She looked up and froze. It was Coop.

Beau, his partner in crime, stepped behind her. Coop pressed a gun into her side.

"Don't make a sound," he hissed. "Here's how it's going to be. You're going to stand up and come with us, quickly and quietly, and nobody gets hurt. But if you try to fight me, we'll open fire."

TEN

Owen watched from across the room as two men escorted Sara out the door. He pressed Juniper into Ruth's arms and turned to Amos.

"The men have found us," he whispered. "Lock the doors and keep everyone inside. They've got Sara, and I'm going after her."

Owen ran for the door, with Amos at his heels. He dashed outside and breathed a sigh of relief to hear the door to the community hall shut behind him. Prayers and panic beat through his heart in equal measure as he rounded the building into a sea of horses, buggies and sleighs. Then he saw Sara, being half led and half dragged through them toward where an ugly blue all-terrain truck sat on the rural highway.

He could feel the weight of the gun hidden at his ankle. Could he risk pausing long enough to reach for it? If he opened fire, would he be putting Sara in even greater danger? They were flanking her so tightly that even if he shot one of the men, the other would be able to kill her before Owen managed to clear a second shot.

"Take me instead!" he shouted. He raised his hands above his head. "Let her go and take me!"

He had no hope of giving them what they wanted, and he knew if they kidnapped him, once they realized that, he wouldn't make it out alive. But it was all he had left.

His life in exchange for Sara's.

The men stopped and looked back at Owen, and for one fleeting moment they turned their attention to him and loosened their grip on her.

And that was when Sara struck.

Her arm swung around defensively. Her elbow caught Coop in the jaw, knocking him to his knees. Beau spun toward her. But it was too late. Sara ran, disappearing into the thin tree line along the side of the road and weaving her way through the pines. Coop fired several times, his bullets splintering the tree trunks and sending the nearby horses whinnying in panic.

Sara was running away from safety. It wouldn't be long until they caught her again. But she was luring the gunmen away from the community hall and the children, including her own baby.

And he'd make sure she wouldn't have to do it alone.

Coop and Beau dashed for their truck. Owen scanned the buggies and sleighs. A tiny two-person sled lay to his left, still tied to its horse. Owen ran for it, yanked it free from its post and leaped in. He flicked the reins, and the horse began to trot. Owen prayed and urged it faster. His eyes locked on Sara's form. She was running parallel to the road using the thin line of trees as her only shelter. The gunmen's truck roared and spun in a circle on the icy road as it turned to follow her. The horse neighed and began to run up a narrow slope and along the fields to Sara's other side. Another gunshot sounded.

Owen grew nearer. In an instant, he'd pull alongside her. He slid over in the seat and steadied the reins with one hand.

"Sara!" he shouted. "I'm on your right!"

She turned and darted toward him. He leaned over and reached out for her. She leaped and grasped hold of his hand. He felt her full weight in his arm. The tiny sleigh bucked beneath him, and for a moment he thought it was about to topple over. Then he leaned back and yanked hard. Sara tumbled into the sled beside him.

"Thank you," she gasped.

"Anytime."

She climbed behind him and around to the seat on his other side. The sled righted. Owen focused on the horizon ahead as the horse ran. The runners skimmed over the snow as if they were flying. He could hear the engine rumbling. The truck was coming up quickly on their left. "We need a plan," Owen said.

"You lure them away from the children!" Sara shouted. "I'll call Seth."

"Agreed. But where do we go?"

She didn't answer. He glanced to his right and saw she'd pulled the cell phone from her pocket. An instant later, he heard her shouting to Seth, filling him in and calling for help.

"He's got us on GPS!" Sara told Owen. "He's looped Jess in too. They've got a whole fleet of law enforcement and emergency vehicles heading our way. We've just got to hang on and stay alive until they get here."

So much for being in hiding. The truck grew closer. He saw with a glance it was a four-wheel drive with off-road tires. If they galloped across the open fields, the

truck could follow. A gunshot whirred through the air
ahead and hit a tree to his left, sending splinters flying
across the path. He could feel the horse's fear and panic
through the reins. The tree line was ending, along with
the meager amount of shelter it provided. Then there
was nothing but empty fields.

*Help me, Lord. Guide us, save us, get us out of here
alive!*

"Sara!" he shouted. "I've got a gun in a holster—"

Then a shimmer of light stole the words from his
lungs. The sun was shining off the ice somewhere below
him on his right. He grew closer. It was a river—frozen over and spreading out like a ribbon through the
snow. Beyond it lay a steep hill, and beyond that the
forest. He gritted his teeth and steered the horse toward
it. They sped down a slope and hit the riverbank—and
then suddenly they were airborne. The sled shook, then
hit hard against the ice, and for a moment it swerved so
hard it nearly flipped. Then the horse stumbled up the
other side of the riverbank and started up the steep hill
there. The truck roared behind them.

Sara looked back and shouted, "They're still coming!"

A loud metallic shriek filled the air, which he knew
in an instant was metal scraping against ice. Then a
crack. He turned back. The frozen crust had given way.
The truck plunged into the lake.

A prayer of thanksgiving began to form on Owen's
lips. The truck had stopped. He and Sara were going
to make it.

Then he heard a bang and felt the sled rip out from

under him. Owen was tossed like a rag doll through the air. His body smacked hard against the snow, knocking the breath from his lungs. His head banged against what felt like a rock. Pain pounded through his skull, and blackness filled his eyes.

"Sara!" he called, but her name slipped from his lips as barely more than a croak.

"I'm okay." Her voice swam from the edges of his aching skull. It sounded like she was breathing hard. "I landed safely. He shot the sled, the skis shattered and we wrecked."

He heard the sounds of the horse knickering and Sara telling it to run. But how had they been shot? The truck had crashed. He opened his eyes; stars filled his view, blocking his vision. The horse had been freed from its reins and was galloping toward the woods for safety. Sara ran for Owen and grabbed his arm.

"Get up!" Desperation filled her voice. "We need to get to cover."

Owen tried to stand, but his legs collapsed beneath him.

"You move one inch, and I'll hurt you so bad you'll wish you were dead!" Coop shouted. Owen looked down the hill. Beau was crouched on the roof of the sinking truck, but Coop was stumbling up the hill with a gun in his hand. "I'm done doing this the nice way, Sara! You're coming with me, and you're going to get me those files! Then I'm going back to that town, and I'm killing your kid and those people for helping you, and there's nothing you can do to stop me."

Owen stumbled in front of Sara and shielded her

with his body. He yanked the gun from his holster and set Coop in his sight. A bullet fired and pain seared through Owen's arm. He'd been shot. The gun fell from his grasp into the snow.

Coop laughed. It was an ugly sound, full of malice.

"Now, get down on your knees and say goodbye to your wife," he said.

Sara breathed a prayer for forgiveness, grabbed the gun and fired twice.

The first shot caught Coop in the shoulder, rendering his arm useless. The second took out his leg, knocking him to the ground. She turned the gun on Beau, who was still crouched on the sinking truck, but before she could fire, he raised his empty hands in surrender.

Sirens filled the air. Law enforcement was racing down the road toward them. Rotors rumbled above. He looked up to see police helicopters.

The gun fell from Sara's fingers. She dropped down beside Owen in the snow, tore a strip off her apron and bound his arm with it.

"You're going to be okay," she said. "It's a through and through. Nothing major was injured."

His other hand reached for her. He longed to hold her, to kiss her face and tell her it was over. Instead he watched as angry tears filled her eyes, and he knew something between them had been broken. Even if he didn't know how to put it into words.

"I'm sorry I didn't tell you about the gun," he said. "I knew you wouldn't like it and would tell me to get rid of it."

"You're right," she replied. "But it's my fault we're

in this mess. And the only way you'll ever be safe is if I leave—now—and never come back."

Rescue and emergency vehicles converged at once from the right, the left and the skies above, cutting short the argument she could tell Owen wanted to have with her. Yes, she was upset he'd been carrying a concealed weapon without telling her. Even more so when she realized it was likely he'd had it on him the whole time they'd been on the run. But that only added to the weight of knowing that she still hadn't filled him in on everything Seth had told her. And her conviction that the only way to save Owen's and Juniper's lives was for her to leave them.

She and Owen were taken to a large highway police station just outside London, Ontario. It had made sense to keep the police out of the loop two days ago, when they didn't know how many corrupt officers were under the thumb of whoever had shot Sara, and in case they needed time to prepare for whatever criminal charges Sara might have laid against her. But now it was too late for that, and it would be impossible to keep the fact she was still alive a secret.

She and Owen were taken in separate vehicles and then sat in separate rooms, which she knew was to keep them from talking and comparing notes. After all, she was a person who, at the very least, would be suspected of faking her own death and had shot a police officer, who no doubt had his own story that painted her as the bad guy. She was thankful she'd just been left by herself in a small interrogation room instead of a jail cell and hadn't been handcuffed.

She hadn't been in there alone more than fifteen minutes when the door opened and Jess walked in carrying Juniper. A cry slipped from Sara's lips as she gathered her baby into her arms and cuddled her, feeling tears of relief fill her eyes.

"Everyone in the town hall is safe and well," Jess said. "Nobody was hurt, thanks to Owen's quick thinking."

"Thank You, God," Sara whispered a prayer of relief under her breath.

"I was actually in town collecting Juniper when your friends Petrus and Hadassah called the community phone," Jess said. "I told them who I was and explained you wanted to know if there was anything you had on you when you were found that you didn't know about. It was only the clothes and the ring though."

Sara nodded. She wasn't surprised, and yet was still disappointed that their last hope of finding out where she'd hidden the files had come up empty.

"Travis is in with Owen now," Jess went on. "He's fine. Paramedics stitched him up and everything's going to be okay. Coop and Beau have been arrested. They were supposed to show up for work today and pulled this instead. They won't be getting out for a long time. Also, provincial police picked up Delia. A gas station cashier called the cops on her when she tried to fill up and drive off without paying."

So all three people who'd physically threatened Sara's life had been caught. But what about the person who'd opened fire at the graveyard and the dentist's office?

"None of them are talking yet," Jess said. "But give them time."

"I'm pretty sure they're all being blackmailed, somehow," Sara said. She thought back to how Delia had been ranting into the phone to whoever had ordered her to kidnap Juniper. "I wouldn't be surprised if the dentist, Dr. Freck, had been blackmailed into falsifying my dental record identification too, and the guy from the funeral home into cremating the body. If only we knew who could possibly have leverage over such a diverse group of people."

And whom she'd apparently had the motivation to steal something from.

"You had no pending criminal charges when you 'died,'" Jess said. "And I don't think you're going to have any pressed against you now. It's pretty clear to all the higher-ups in law enforcement that there's something seriously wrong going on here, and they're putting their full resources behind wrapping this up and catching whoever's behind this."

But who knew how long that would take? Until then, Owen and Juniper would still be in danger.

"Seth said he had contacts in Pennsylvania Dutch Country who might be able to hide me," Sara said. "I'd like to make arrangements to go into hiding right away, as soon as I'm done being questioned."

Jess's eyes widened. "But we've got three criminals in custody. We're able to protect you here in Canada."

"But there's nothing to stop whoever's behind this from sending more people after me," Sara said. "I'm their target. Not Owen. Maybe if I leave, Owen and Juniper will finally be safe."

There was another knock on the door as police officers came in to take her statement. Thankfully, they let her keep Juniper with her. Even as she cuddled her precious baby in her arms, she knew that she couldn't—she wouldn't—take Juniper with her. She couldn't take her away from Owen. He was an excellent father who had built his life around caring for their little girl. And Travis and Jess would be there to help protect them both.

It took a couple of hours to give her statement. She took her time answering the cops' questions and being as thorough as possible, telling them every little piece of information she knew. Once she walked out that door and disappeared over the border, there was no way of knowing when she'd even return to Canada or how hard it would be for the cops to contact her for further questioning.

Finally the questioning was done, and the only thing left to do was to say the hardest goodbye she could ever imagine having to say.

It was late afternoon when she finally walked out the front door of the police station. Waiting for her in the parking lot, were three large and identical black cars. She'd be making her way across the border to Pennsylvania in a three-vehicle convoy, Jess explained. She'd ride in one car with an undercover law enforcement officer. Two unmarked police cars would follow at an inconspicuous distance.

In the meantime, friends of Jess and Travis would start strategically planting messages through the dark web aimed at letting whoever was listening know that Sara had left the country. The convoy would make a couple of strategic stops on the other side of the American border where Sara—in modern clothes—would be picked up by security cameras and safely seen by witnesses, in order to back up that story for anyone looking into it.

"Then you'll completely disappear off the map," Jess said, "with the last known traces of you being somewhere in the Midwest. Both law enforcement and dark web channels will know that you're no longer in Canada."

"Thank you," Sara said.

"I still think you should stay," Jess said. "But they'll take good care of you and keep you safe."

Sara nodded, forcing back the hot tears she could feel building at the backs of her eyes.

"I want you to take Juniper to Owen," she told Jess, "and tell him I've gone, and that as soon as I can, I'll send word that I've arrived safely."

"Where are you going?" Owen's voice came from behind her.

She turned to see him walking down the front steps of the police station toward her. He'd changed into a clean sweatshirt and jeans. A soft sling bandaged his right arm where he'd been shot. His green eyes flicked toward the three black cars and he frowned. Jess excused herself. Owen's left hand brushed Sara's shoulder, silently guiding her to a more secluded area around the side of the building where they could talk without being overheard.

"What do you think you're doing?" he asked. "Are you actually trying to run away to the United States without saying goodbye?"

"I'm leaving Juniper with you," she said. She stretched her arms out and practically pushed their daughter into his free arm. He took her. "You're an incredible father, and I know you'll take the best care of her."

He shook his head. "This is ridiculous. You're not just running away from me—again—and trying to solve whatever problems we're dealing with alone."

"You're not going with me," she said. "I'm the target. Whoever is behind this is after me. If I go, you and Juniper will be safe—"

"You can't possibly know that—"

"Our daughter needs you. The residents of Kilpatrick need you."

"And what about us?" he said. "We don't need each other?"

"There is no us!" Her voice rose, and he rocked back on his heels. "Maybe there was once. Seth told me I was in an elite training program to do spycraft overseas. That's how my subconscious knows how to fight a bad guy and disarm a threat. And apparently I turned down promotions and assignments after I met you because I didn't want to leave you."

His eyes widened. "You told me you'd turned down assignments, but you never made it sound like a big deal or told me it was because of us. Maybe things would've turned out differently if you had."

"Maybe," she conceded. "I don't know. Just like we don't know what would've happened if you'd been honest with me about how you felt about your future. But then apparently I changed. I did horrible things—"

He stepped toward her and cut her off. "And whatever it is you did, I refuse to believe it was that bad."

"I tried to take Juniper away from you!" The words flew out of her mouth in a rush before he could interrupt. "That's what Delia told me yesterday that had me so upset, and what I asked Seth to look into. I asked

Casey to draw up legal papers that stripped you of your parental rights, turned your finances inside out, and stopped you from going near me or our daughter ever again!"

His face paled as if she'd physically punched him.

"No," he said. "No, that's not possible. The Sara I knew would never have done that."

"Except apparently I did," Sara said. "Seth talked to Casey and confirmed it."

She watched as emotions washed over his face in cascading waves of anger, confusion and pain. She remembered how he'd looked at her back at the grave-yard—with frustration bordering on disgust—before he'd realized she'd forgotten her memory.

"That's why you can't give up your life to hide in Pennsylvania with me," she said. "What if we're off the grid together, I suddenly get my memories back and you're trapped there with a woman who'd do some-thing so loathsome and hurt you? What if I took Juniper and suddenly became the kind of person who wanted to stop you from ever seeing her again?" A sob choked her throat. "That's why I can't let you or Juniper go with me. I care about you too much to risk hurting you ever again."

He understood, right? That she was doing this to protect him? That she cared about him far more than she knew how to put into words? She searched Owen's gaze, looking for understanding. Maybe even the prom-ise that they'd find a way to stay in touch.

But instead, she watched as the light in his eyes dimmed, just as completely as if he'd closed the shutters on a lantern.

"I was wrong," he said stiffly. "Apparently it is possible you've done things I don't know if I can forgive you for. Goodbye, Sara. Safe travels."

He paused long enough for her to brush a goodbye kiss over their daughter's head. Then he turned away and walked back to the police station before he could see her tears.

A few moments later, Jess came back out, escorted Sara over to the cars and introduced her to the undercover officers. Sara hugged her goodbye and climbed in the back of a car, and the convoy pulled out. They'd provided her with a warm blanket for her legs and a bag of supplies, none of which she ever remembered seeing before. The officer told her it would take two hours to reach the United States border. After they crossed, they'd stop at a safe house, where she'd get changed into entirely new clothing and change her hair, then they'd continue for another two days to reach their final destination.

"Be prepared to turn over any personal items that could be used to identify you," he warned her.

Her fingers reached for the gold ring she still wore around her neck.

Sara Owen Kilpatrick.

Those words were once her only link to her identity. Then they became her only hope for saving her life. Now they were a reminder of everything she'd lost forever.

She closed her eyes.

Lord, help me to forgive myself for the choices I made in the past and the person I was. Whoever I've been and whatever I've done, I turn the whole of myself over to

You. Help me trust in Your forgiveness. Surround Owen and Juniper with Your love.

Tears filled her eyes, red-hot against the cold wintery air around her. She reached into her pocket for a handkerchief and felt a soft square of fabric against her fingertips. She pulled it out. It was the same scrap of cloth she'd had in her pocket when Petrus had found her. She hadn't paid much attention to it back at the *grossdaadi* house, but now she could see it was perfectly square, like the quilts she'd made with Hadassah or the blanket Juniper had been bundled in when she'd handed her over to Owen all those months ago.

A memory hit her like a flood. She could feel the hard plastic of the memory card against her fingers, the soft fleece of the fabric and the sharp prick of the needle against her finger.

"Stop!" She leaned forward and jabbed the undercover officer in the shoulder. "I have to go back! Now!"

ELEVEN

Owen tapped his razor against the side of the bath-room sink of his small apartment above the hardware store and splashed cold water on his face. He looked at his reflection in the mirror. Shaving left-handed had taken twice as long as usual. His right hand was still in a sling, and he couldn't remember the last time he'd been clean-shaven. But something about the way he'd said goodbye to Sara made him want to get rid of the last reminders of married life instead of waiting for his moustache to grow in. Then he collected a sleeping Juniper from his bedroom and carefully carried her downstairs to his office, where he laid her gently in her crib.

Had Sara been right in believing that once she was gone from his and Juniper's lives the threats against them would stop? Certainly Travis and Jess had assured him that both law enforcement and any criminals trying to track Sara on the dark web would know she was gone.

But still they'd gotten a friend to install bullet-proof glass in both the hardware store and apartment's windows. They'd also set up extra security cameras to monitor the street outside the store which could be monitored by Owen, Travis, Jess and Seth remotely. They'd also worked out a series of complex security code words Owen could use to alert Travis and Jess if there was any sign of trouble.

When they hadn't been making strategic plans to ramp up security around Owen and Juniper's small home, the drive from the London police station back to Kilpatrick with Travis and Jess had been mostly silent. A grief as deep and complicated as the one he'd felt when he thought Sara had died pressed down on him like a weighted blanket. Seth had been waiting at the house with Owen's cell phone and truck, and let him know the horse and buggy they'd borrowed had been returned safely to their owner. The horse they'd used for their rescue had found his way home, and Amos had already offered to help the owner repair the damaged sled. Seth was staying at the Tatlows for dinner, and both Jess and Travis invited Owen to stay at their home for as long as he wanted, especially since their three kids would be home that night as well.

But he'd wanted to be alone. Seeing their caring and concerned faces only reminded him of what had happened with Sara.

Owen's cell phone had started chiming as soon as he'd turned it on. It was filled with messages from various people in the community about the winter fair. It had started ringing before he'd even made it home, so he'd turned it off and stuffed it in his pocket.

Any new calls that came in could wait.

A floorboard creaked from deep within the hardware store. Owen leaped to his feet, his heart thudding. Was it Sara? Had she somehow made her way back here? Was she in danger?

"Hello?" he called.

"Owen!" Roger's deep voice boomed from the other room. "So you are here! What did you do to your arm?"

What was the mayor-elect doing in his store after hours? How had he even gotten in?

"Long story short, I injured it after I had an accident with a horse and needed a few stitches," Owen said. "What are you doing here?"

Roger's large form filled the doorway separating his store from his office. "Hope you don't mind me popping by unannounced. People have been calling you all day about wanting to get deposits down for some of the vendors and entertainment for the winter fair, but nobody could find you."

"I was out of town for a couple days," Owen said truthfully. "Visiting a small town in southern Ontario and getting some inspiration about how we could do things differently here. The town's already in debt, and people want to shell out even more money on these vendors and entertainers you mentioned. Maybe there's a way to cut costs and yet still celebrate the winter fair by getting back to our roots."

Was it his imagination, or did a scowl flicker across Roger's face for a moment before snapping back to his regular smile?

"How did you get in here?" Owen asked.

Roger shrugged. "Door was unlocked."

"No, it wasn't," Owen said. "I'd have noticed if it was."

"Okay, you got me!" Roger raised his hands in mock surrender. "I got a spare set of keys to the place when your cousin was considering selling me the place as a real estate deal."

Real estate deal? Roger had told Owen he had multiple business interests, but he hadn't known buying buildings was one of them.

"Can you keep your voice down? Juniper's asleep."

Roger pressed a large finger to his lips. "I wanted to leave you a note to let you know people were worried about you," he added in a mock whisper. "People have been worried about the recent crime situation around here. There've been two random shootings recently. Our dentist died, and our mortician is in the hospital. You can't blame people for wanting to hear from their mayor. I've been reassuring people that once I'm sworn in, I'll be hiring a state-of-the-art private security team to help keep Kilpatrick safe."

Spending more money they didn't have.

"Or you could find a way to better resource our local police," Owen said. "We could also start a community watch. There are so many wonderful people who live here. We need to do more to look out for each other."

"You mean like that woman you've been seen around town with?" Roger asked pointedly. He glanced around the room as if he was in a stage play. "Where do you have her hiding?"

"She left the country," Owen said. "I don't know if or when she'll be back."

"Pity. And what did she think of our little town?"

"She helped me come up with some great ideas to revitalize it."

"Oh really?" Roger said. Owen hadn't been paying attention to the fact he was still standing behind his desk and Roger was in the middle of his office. But now Roger crossed the floor, coming closer until they were face-to-face. He leaned both hands on the desk as if wanting to push it into the ground. "What kind of ideas did she come up with?" Something rumbled in his voice, like a large grizzly bear that wasn't used to being challenged.

Instinctively, Owen tried to cross his arms, but thanks to the sling he could only tuck one beside the other. His chest rose.

"Your voice is getting loud again," Owen said, keeping his own tone level and calm. "They weren't her ideas, actually. They were mine." It was just that having her near helped him see things in a whole new way. "I want to take the winter fair back to what it was like when I was a kid. Before we worried about spending our money to bring in outsiders and instead focused on what made our own community great. Like a local jam-making competition, pony rides and a talent show. Things that celebrate us."

A grin rose on Roger's mouth that reminded Owen of an animal baring his teeth. "Well, some folks are going to be mighty disappointed to hear that."

"I reckon people will get over the disappointment a lot faster than they would losing their town to debt," Owen said.

"Too bad you won't be mayor for much longer," Roger said.

"True. But I've already decided I'm going to run again when you're up for reelection. And in the meantime, I can use that time to find other ways to help build up my hometown. I still own the title on more than a few unused buildings in this town, and I want to see about opening some of them up for people to get a few town activities going, like a library, some free adult-education classes and a food bank. Maybe I'll start some community groups focused on issues like cutting our debt and restoring Main Street to its former glory, and hold some town meetings to see what ideas people have. Really listen to what people who live here want this town to be.

"Did you know that some tourist company tried to buy up Main Street a little over a year ago and turn us into some tacky tourist trap? If we keep going this way, next time a vulture company like that comes back, we won't be in any position to say no, and it'll be able to pick us off for scraps. But if we all pull together, maybe we'll be strong enough to save our town and fight them off."

Roger barked out a laugh, louder than Owen would've liked. Juniper began to fuss in her crib with that little cry that let him know she wasn't sure yet if she was going to wake up or fall back to sleep. Then Roger's eyes narrowed. "Sounds like an awfully busy little bee for a man who didn't want to be mayor."

"You mean a man who took his time to think, pray and listen to the folks in this town before deciding he wanted to be mayor," Owen said. "I've never been much for snap decisions. Guess you're gonna have to get used to me buzzing around for the next few years, because I'm going to do my best to keep you on your toes and make sure the plans you make are what's best for this town and the people who live here."

Owen hadn't actually meant the words as a challenge. But as he spoke, he could feel fresh resolve filling his core. Yes, this was who he was. This was what he wanted. He only wished Sara were here to see it.

Then he saw the anger in Roger's eyes. Roger took two big steps back from the table, his white-knuckled hands clenching into fists.

"Well," Roger said, "some might say it's risky to go poking around in another man's business. I hope you know what you're doing."

"Oh, I'm sure I do," Owen said. "So you can throw all the fancy parties you want, filling people's heads with shiny ideas that are bad for this town." How could he have not realized Roger was the one who'd stirred up and then steered the conversation that had gotten people all worked up? His personality was too powerful for anything else. "I'm going to be here, with my hands in the soil, planting good seeds in this town when they get back down to earth."

Footsteps creaked on the floorboards in the store again. Owen's heart leaped into his throat as time seemed to freeze.

It was Sara.

She was here. She was back.

Sara was still dressed in the Amish garb he'd last seen her in. But her bonnet had fallen down her back and her hair streamed loose around her face. Suddenly he wanted to run across the floor to her, gather her in his arms and tell her he'd never let her leave again.

Instead, he watched as Roger turned toward her, his hand outstretched to shake hers.

"Oh, you're back," he said. "I don't think we've been properly introduced. I'm Roger, the mayor-elect."

Owen watched as Sara's face paled. Her beautiful eyes went wide, and her lower lip began to tremble.

"I remember you," she whispered.

And Owen knew without a doubt that Sara was looking into the eyes of the man who'd tried to kill her.

Sara's blood froze in her veins, and she felt her legs threaten to collapse beneath her as she stared into the face of the man who had tried to end her life. His voice had been the roaring boom she'd heard behind her as she'd run. He'd been the one who'd threatened her, shot her and called her a thief.

But how could she convince Owen that Roger was the man behind it all? He had no reason to trust her. Not on this. Not on anything. And she had no proof.

She took a deep breath and tried to will herself to say something. She could hear Juniper fussing quietly in her crib, like a tiny engine trying to pick up steam.

Owen just stood there with one hand in his pocket and the other in the sling.

"Well, this is a surprise," he started. "I didn't expect to see you here today." Then he blinked as his phone rang in his pocket. He pulled his hand out and glanced at the screen. "Wow, I'm sorry, guys—I've got to take this. Just hang tight. I won't be half a second."

Then Owen walked past her, and his good arm brushed against hers. He disappeared through the door she'd just walked through and back into the store.

"Hey!" Owen's voice floated in from the other room. "Yeah, I'm in the store now. Just calling about those nail order we discussed. There's something wrong with the shipment and I need help sorting it out."

Owen had left her alone in his office with the man who'd wanted her dead. Roger stepped toward her. The large man's gaze fixed on her like a hunter setting a deer in his sights.

"I hear you've lost your memory," he said. "You poor little thing. I can't imagine how terrifying that must be."

"Mamamammmamama." The sound of Juniper babbling drew Sara's gaze past him to the crib. Her baby girl was standing up and holding tight to the side of her crib.

Swiftly, Sara crossed the room, scooped her up and bundled her in the quilt she had sewn for her before she'd lost her memories. Slowly, Sara's fingers ran along the edges, feeling for the memory card.

Owen's voice rose from the other room. It sounded like he'd gone from talking about nails to something about a hammer.

"Here, let me hold her," the mayor-elect said. Roger stretched out his arms toward Juniper. Instinctively, Sara took a step back. The large man chuckled, like he enjoyed seeing her discomfort. "Oh, don't be like that. I'm just going to hold her for a moment. I'm not going to hurt her."

His voice was as sickly sweet as corn syrup. It was like he was testing her. Like a large truck playing chicken with a horse and buggy on a narrow road. Or a large child waving his fist a few inches from the nose of a smaller one to see if he'd flinch.

"Come on," he said. "Just one little cuddle. Unless you've got some good reason why I can't hold your baby?"

Not one that she had proof of. Not one that she knew how to make Owen believe.

Desperately, her fingers searched the blanket seams, feeling for the card and praying her memory had been right.

"Because it would be pretty dangerous for a girl in your position to start making claims she can't back up with facts," Roger added. "Especially when everybody knows her mind is gone."

"Not one step closer," she said. "I know where the files are."

He stepped back, and for a fleeting moment she watched as fear crossed his face. Then his eyes narrowed, something evil turned on his lips and the last remaining shred of his jovial mask fell from his face, leaving nothing but anger and fury behind.

"So what?" he asked. "You still think you can threaten me?"

She'd threatened him? Roger's voice took on a high and mocking tone.

"'Oh, leave my poor Owen alone or else I'll tell everyone the truth about you!'" he said, clearly pretending to be her. "What truth? That I'm kind enough to give people loans they can't repay? That I have my fingers in more pies than I let on? It's called business, you child."

Juniper whimpered and snuggled deeper into Sara's arms. Sara ran one protective hand down her daughter's back and felt a small, hard object buried deep inside the quilt's center seam.

"I needed everyone to believe you were dead so that Owen's assets didn't get tied up in legal proceedings while police searched for you," Roger said, "A man with a missing soon-to-be ex-wife can't sell or leverage his properties without a few eyebrows being raised. But you just had to come back, didn't you?

"So now, you are going to stay out of my business and keep your pretty little mouth shut about it," Roger said. "You're going to hand over my files and apologize for tricking my assistant into handing them over. And then you're going to become my biggest fan. You'll be sweet and polite, and tell Owen how much you love all my ideas, and serve me lemonade and cookies whenever I come over to visit. You're going to hope every day that I am a nice enough man to forget about this." He pulled his jacket open just enough to show her the gun tucked into his waistband. "Now show me you're going to behave by letting me hold your baby. Or I promise I will do things that will leave you with memories you'll wish you were able to forget."

His large fingertips wrapped around her wrist and twisted. Pain shot through her. Tears filled her eyes.

Owen's voice rose from behind Roger like an ocean's roar.

"Get away from my wife!"

TWELVE

Roger dropped her wrist and spun, just as Owen swung his left arm around like a player at bat. Something cracked against Roger's jaw and the man fell back, and only then did Sara realize what weapon he was wielding. It was the giant tactical flashlight.

Roger stumbled to his feet. Vile threats dripped from his mouth.

"Owen!" Sara shouted. "He has a gun!"

The weapon flashed in Roger's hand. But before he could fire, Owen latched on to it like a wolf protecting his den from a charging bear. Roger swore and thrashed, leveling blow after blow against Owen, trying to get him to let go of the gun. But Owen held firm.

"I'm not going to let you hurt my family."

Footsteps pounded through the store. Jess and Travis rushed in.

"Police!" Jess shouted. Her badge was on a lanyard around her neck, and her gun was steady in her hands. "Roger Wilson. I'm arresting you on the charge of attempted murder of Sara Kilpatrick."

Within moments, Owen and Travis had Roger subdued and handcuffed.

Sirens sounded, filling the air. It sounded like a fleet of law enforcement was on its way.

Owen rushed to Sara. He threw his good arm around her and pulled her close. She wrapped her free arm around him and hugged him back, with their daughter bundled between them. Owen's lips brushed the tears from her cheeks. He buried his head in her hair.

"It's okay," he whispered. "I've got you. You're safe. He's going away. He's never going to hurt you again."

She looked up into his face. "How did they know?"

"They have remote access to the store's video security feed," he said, "so they knew he'd let himself in. I also worked out a series of code words with them in case of an emergency."

"You were on the phone with them?" she asked, as understanding dawned. "You were talking to Travis and Jess this whole time?"

He hadn't abandoned her after all. He'd been planning her rescue.

The sirens grew louder. Red and blue lights flashed against the windows.

"Yeah, of course." He nodded. "Nail was code that we were in danger and they needed to move in. Hammer referred to the person who'd tried to kill you."

"But how did you know I'd remembered Roger was the one who'd shot me?" she asked.

He chuckled softly and his voice grew husky in his throat. "I could see it in your eyes, and that was all I needed."

They pulled away from each other as a dozen more uniformed officers poured into Owen's office. Roger was dragged out, swearing and threatening retribution, back through the store into the waiting police car.

"You okay?" Jess asked.

Sara nodded. "We're good. Can you give us a moment?"

Jess signaled to the remaining officers, and they filed out, leaving Owen, Sara and Juniper alone again. Sara eased Juniper into Owen's arms, took the blanket and headed for the desk.

"I found the memory card." She stretched the blanket out on the desk, then reached into the drawer and grabbed a pair of scissors. "I was right that I'd sewn it into fabric. But it wasn't my clothes. It was this blanket. The files had been here with you for safekeeping all along."

She slit the seam of the blanket and reached inside. There lay a small memory card, inside a waterproof plastic box and wrapped in plastic. Whatever was on the card, she apparently hadn't wanted to risk it being damaged.

She pried it out of the protective casing, held it up between her fingers and took a deep breath. "And here it is. We're about to find the answers to all our questions—what I did and why."

It was time to see what she'd nearly lost her life for. She took two steps toward the computer. But then she felt Owen's hand on her elbow. His fingers tugged her gently to stop.

"Wait," Owen said, and she turned to face him. "Before we plug that memory card into the computer and see what's in those files, there's something important I need to tell you."

His fingers intertwined with hers.

"I love you, Sara," he said, "and I'm going to keep on loving you regardless of any mistakes you've made or things you might've done that hurt me. You are the woman I love, and you always have been, even on days when loving you hurt so bad it was almost too much to bear."

He leaned forward. So did she, and her forehead gently rested against his. They stayed there for one long moment, with their daughter between them and their breaths intermingling.

"I love you too," she whispered. "But I'm scared of what I'll find."

"Me too. But we're in this together."

Their lips gently met for a brief and fleeting kiss. Then they pulled back and walked around to the computer together.

She pulled up a chair beside his, and they sat. He turned the computer on and entered his password. She pushed the memory card into the slot, reached for the mouse and clicked the folder that appeared on the screen. Dozens of files spilled out. There were financial documents, real estate deals and loan arrangements as spreadsheet after spreadsheet filled the screen. Before she had time to wonder what they meant, a video file opened on the screen and began to play.

She watched as the Sara she once was leaned forward, pushed a button on a computer and then sat back in her chair and faced the screen.

The former Sara looked older somehow. Her black hair was cropped short and stylish, with subtle highlights of a pretty amber gold. She wore a navy blue blazer, and while her makeup was impeccable, it did nothing to hide the fatigue in her eyes.

"Owen, please give me a minute and don't turn this off," the Sara on the screen said. Then she took a deep breath and started again. "Owen, hi. I have something I need to tell you."

"She's practicing," Owen whispered. "It's like this is the first draft of a message she—you—hadn't decided how to send."

The Sara in real life reached for Owen's hand and took it.

"I know you have no reason to trust me," the Sara on the screen said. "I've made a mess of things, but to be fair, you have too." She checked herself and tried again. "I know you might not trust me. But I think you're in serious trouble. I don't think your cousin's hit-and-run was an accident, and now the person behind his death is trying to come after you."

Her voice hitched.

"When your cousin died you told me that a company tried to buy Kilpatrick from him and turn it into a tourist trap I was curious so I did a bit of digging online," she said. "It turns out that company's address is nothing more than a post office box and its phone number just rings through to a voicemail box.

"Now, I've been working a lot of cases involving money laundering by overseas drug lords. And something about this whole situation reminded me of the tactics they use. I wondered if the buyer was using a shell company to hide his identity. I dug deeper and found out the company was owned by Roger Wilson. Turns out Roger owns a lot of different real estate and loan companies. A contact at the RCMP Financial Crimes division confirmed they are looking into him, but that cases like that can take years before there's even an indictment. And considering the fact he's supposed to become mayor in a few months I don't think we have any time to waste."

She blew out a long breath and ran her fingers through her hair.

"A few weeks ago, I realized Roger was following me," she went on. "He just kept showing up places where I was. When I confronted him, he chuckled and asked me to join him for drinks. When I told him I wasn't interested, he told me that you'd inherited some pretty valuable property, and he'd like to buy it.

"He said we could do this the easy way or the hard way. The easy way would be that I ensure I get the properties he wants from you in the divorce and sell them to him for a generous price. The hard way involved him using his 'business dealings' to bankrupt the town and foreclose on the properties once they were worthless. He was pretty vague about how exactly he was going to do this. And I tried to talk to you about it, but you wouldn't listen, so I started pulling together evidence to prove it to you—"

"I do remember you saying something about not trusting Roger and seeing him in Ottawa," Owen said, "but I never realized…"

His voice trailed off as the Sara on the screen went on.

"I decided to pretend to play his game to see what I could get of his business records," she said, "I got Casey to write up some nonsense documents pretending I was accusing you of stealing from me and pretending

I wanted sole custody of Juniper. Then I showed them to one of his assistants, told him I was going after sole ownership of the Kilpatrick properties and I needed to know his company's financial details for due diligence.

"Only he sent me a lot more than he should have. Because it looks like there's really bad stuff here that could prove he's intentionally lending people money they can't pay back in order to foreclose on their properties or even blackmail them. I won't know for sure until I've sifted through it all. The Canadian military intelligence has no jurisdiction over crimes that take place inside our borders, but once I know what I've got I'm going to pass it on to the federal Financial Crimes unit. Maybe there's something there that will help them catch this guy.

"But in the meantime, please, don't let him get his hooks into Kilpatrick. Don't let any of his shell companies loan the town or its residents money. And you just can't let this guy become mayor. He'll destroy your hometown."

A tiny cry rose from somewhere off-screen, and Sara realized it was a newborn Juniper crying. The video ended. And for a long moment, Sara and Owen sat there, looking at their reflections mingling with the files on the screen.

Owen found his voice first.

"I'm so sorry I didn't listen when you tried to warn me about Roger," he said. "Or realize your life was in danger."

"Maybe I got so upset and defensive I let myself get derailed without actually trying to tell you what you needed to know," Sara said.

"Neither of us were very good at communicating back then," he said. "Every conversation we tried to have seemed to turn to a fight. But now we not only have the proof we need to solidify the case against Roger, we also know that you didn't steal government files or military secrets. It sounds like you didn't do anything criminal, steal any files or even break the law. You just tricked someone who worked for Roger into giving you information nobody was supposed to find."

She ran her fingers along his jaw and turned his face toward hers.

"Now we know that I never tried to hurt you or take Juniper from you," she said. "Whatever mistakes I made, I was trying to protect you."

Snow fell gently against the darkened windows of the Tatlow's farmhouse. A fire crackled in the living room fireplace. Sara sat alone in the armchair, nestled her sleeping baby in her arms and listened to the chorus of excited voices spilling through the doorway from the kitchen.

Jess, Travis, Seth and Owen were on a video chat with their citizen detective contacts, excitedly going over all the details of the unraveling case as it unspooled before them.

When word got out that Roger was in police custody, Officers Coop and Beau, Delia, and the cop who'd planted drugs in the Tatlows' farmhouse were falling over each other to confess that he was the man who'd blackmailed them into "doing him a small favor" in escalating attacks on Sara in the hopes of getting the files on the memory card back. In exchange, Roger had promised to cancel hundreds of thousands of dollars they owed to various dodgy financial businesses of his. Derek had regained consciousness and confirmed Roger had been leaning on his parents too. Dr. Freck also turned out to owe money to Roger.

But in the first surprising twist of the case, the autopsy showed the drugs that killed him had already been in his system when he'd left Roger's party, and multiple witnesses confirmed Roger had been the one who'd fixed the dentist's drink.

As surprising as that was, it didn't come close to Bert's discovery that the officer assigned to investigate the hit-and-run death of Owen's cousin almost a year ago had also owed Roger a lot of money. The officer had destroyed evidence that Roger had been behind the hit-and-run too.

Finally, after Derek told them where he'd hidden the ashes of the woman found dead in Sara's car, the DNA sample led back to a missing-person case from a few months ago. The woman had been living on the streets, and witnesses confirmed that Roger was the man whose car they'd seen her getting into. Now Roger had been charged with her murder.

Sara closed her eyes and prayed.

Lord, so many unexplained loose threads all tied into one man's incredible greed, and so many people were hurt because of his selfishness. Thank You for all the people working together to bring him to justice. Thank You for saving my life and bringing Owen, Juniper and all our friends through it safely. Please give peace to his victims and their families. For You are able to redeem all things.

She opened her eyes and looked up as Owen slipped through the door and into the living room.

"Is she sleeping?" he whispered.

"Yes."

"Do you want me to take her so that you can go back in the meeting?" he asked.

She shook her head. "To be honest, I'm exhausted and overwhelmed. I know I used to be the kind of person who tried to do it all by herself. But right now I'm comforted knowing there's a huge team working on this puzzle together."

"Okay, how about I put her to bed and we go for a walk?"

She felt a smile cross her lips. "Sounds perfect."

He took Juniper from her arms and brought her upstairs to her crib. He was back a few moments later. They put on their boots and coats, and she took his gloved hand in hers, and they slipped outside into the wintery night. The sky was deep blue and fathomless above them, dotted with tiny lights.

She took in a long, deep and cleansing breath, letting the cold, clean air fill her lungs.

Their fingers linked, and they walked away from the farmhouse. The noise and the distraction of the conversations and the house disappeared in the distance until there was nothing but the sky above, the glittering snow beneath her and the handsome man by her side.

"I've decided to stay on as mayor," Owen said finally, breaking the silence. "But I'm going to push for the formation of a town council and also that we have a proper election in the fall. As much as I want to help mold and shape this town, I want to earn it, through my ideas and by getting people on board. Our financials had gotten so bad we were on the verge of falling apart, and getting back on track is going to mean everyone working together."

"Why am I not surprised?" she said.

"Because you know me so well." He stopped walking. So did she, and he turned to face her. "Also I want to build a house, somewhere in town, for you, me and Juniper to live in together as a family. If you'll have me."

Happiness filled her chest until she thought it would burst.

"Don't forget you also need to get the snowmobile from the pond when it thaws and try to rebuild it," she said.

"True," Owen said with a grin. "Look, I don't know if you want to continue with the *plain* way of life or how that would work out. Certainly Dr. Amos found a way that worked for him and his family. I don't know if you're going to want to return to work one day or what kind of work you're going to want to do. Or what's going to happen as your memories keep returning."

"Neither do I," she admitted.

"But I know that whatever happens, I want us to go through it together," he said. "As a family and as a team. The biggest mistake we ever made was trying to go through the tough stuff alone. And I don't ever want to make that mistake again."

Then Owen dropped to one knee in the snow in front of her.

"Sara, you once told me you didn't need a marriage proposal. But what I've realized is that I did. I needed to choose. I needed to put my heart in my hands and ask you to take it."

Her heart caught in her throat as the happiness that had been building in her chest burst like sparklers through her veins.

"Please marry me again, Sara," he said. "Let's renew our vows. Right now. Tonight. I've fallen in love with you twice, and no matter what the future brings, I want to face it together and keep falling in love with you every day, again and again, for the rest of my life."

"Yes," she said. "Yes, of course, Owen. I will be your wife, and you'll be my husband. Tonight and forever."

He leaped to his feet, then his hands reached around her neck, unclasped the chain and took off the ring. He slid it onto her finger. Then he swept her up into his arms, and she felt her feet leave the ground.

She wrapped her arms around his neck. He kissed her lips, and she kissed him back.

And she knew whatever the future brought, they'd face it together.

* * * * *

If you enjoyed this story, look for these other books by Maggie K. Black:

Witness Protection Unraveled
Christmas Witness Conspiracy

Dear Reader,

I live in Canada just outside Toronto, and this summer my amazing daughter and I discovered the adventure and joy of taking "mystery road trips."

It starts with a package arriving in the mail. Inside is a series of beautiful brown envelopes wrapped in twine. We'd open the first one and head to the coordinates on the map. After exploring the area, we'd open the envelope to the next.

We visited waterfalls, beaches and cafés. We discovered an incredible rural art installation and the small town where a popular television show is filmed. On one trip, we even saw a wolf.

On our third trip, to my surprise, we visited an Amish market. Buggies and cars sat side by side in the parking lot. I got lost in wonder exploring the food, clothing, books and maps of Pennsylvania Dutch Country.

As we drove away, the idea for this book started brewing in my mind.

Thank you again for joining me on this journey. I love writing these books, and each one is a new adventure.

Maggie

LISCNM1222

Get 4 FREE REWARDS!

We'll send you 2 FREE Books plus 2 FREE Mystery Gifts.

FREE
Value Over
$20

Both the **Love Inspired®** and **Love Inspired®** Suspense series feature compelling novels filled with inspirational romance, faith, forgiveness, and hope.

YES! Please send me 2 FREE novels from the Love Inspired or Love Inspired Suspense series and my 2 FREE gifts (gifts are worth about $10 retail). After receiving them, if I don't wish to receive any more books, I can return the shipping statement marked "cancel." If I don't cancel, I will receive 6 brand-new Love Inspired Larger-Print books or Love Inspired Suspense Larger-Print books every month and be billed just $6.24 each in the U.S. or $6.49 each in Canada. That is a savings of at least 17% off the cover price. It's quite a bargain! Shipping and handling is just 50¢ per book in the U.S. and $1.25 per book in Canada.* I understand that accepting the 2 free books and gifts places me under no obligation to buy anything. I can always return a shipment and cancel at any time by calling the number below. The free books and gifts are mine to keep no matter what I decide.

Choose one: ☐ **Love Inspired**
Larger-Print
(122/322 IDN GRDF)

☐ **Love Inspired Suspense**
Larger-Print
(107/307 IDN GRDF)

Name (please print)

Address   Apt. #

City   State/Province   Zip/Postal Code

Email: Please check this box ☐ if you would like to receive newsletters and promotional emails from Harlequin Enterprises ULC and its affiliates. You can unsubscribe anytime.

Mail to the Harlequin Reader Service:
IN U.S.A.: P.O. Box 1341, Buffalo, NY 14240-8531
IN CANADA: P.O. Box 603, Fort Erie, Ontario L2A 5X3

Want to try 2 free books from another series? Call 1-800-873-8635 or visit www.ReaderService.com.

HARLEQUIN
PLUS

Announcing a **BRAND-NEW** multimedia subscription service for romance fans like you!

Read, Watch and Play.

Experience the easiest way to get the romance content you crave.

Start your **FREE 7 DAY TRIAL** at
<u>www.harlequinplus.com/freetrial</u>.

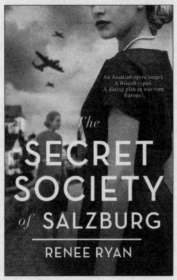